MOMENTS

Enjoy

Ebony Dawn

MOMENTS

BY

EBONY DAWN

Bookstand
Publishing
www.BookstandPublishing.com

Published by
Bookstand Publishing
Houston, TX 77079
2008_4

ISBN 1-58909-351-8

Printed in the United States of America

Preface

Life
Awesome, magnificent and especially perplexing in it's relentless quest for change while auspiciously remaining the same in essence. The struggles, conquests and joys are paralleled to the coquettish innocence of spring to the bold selfish arrogance of summer to the full-bloomed beauty and sophistication of autumn to the final culmination of wisdom, resignation and understanding of winter.
…Life and nature, the total complement.

Acknowledgements

From Pat Ebron (Ebony Dawn)

To my family,

Clarence B. Wilson, my father, Marie Wilson, my mother, Anita Ross, my sister and Raymond B Wilson, my brother. I thank you all for my wonderful childhood. Although my father and brother are no longer with me in life, they are still a vivid part of my memories of "the good old days".

My new "good old days" are being formed by,

William B. Ebron, my husband, Kerin Anderson-Johnson, my first born, Karla M Anderson, my baby (forever) and my grandchildren, Sage, my precious darling, Cheyanne, my little pumpkin head and Sean, my little man.

I love you all and I thank you for the many, many joys that life can bring.

Table of Contents

Before the Dawn

I awoke to the sound of "Earth Wind and Fire" playing loudly in the background. I looked around my bedroom. The things that were so familiar to me were suddenly closing in. I was suffocating. Dying from boredom.

I heard Jeff and Sylvia, my teenage children practicing a dance routine. They practiced every Saturday morning for the Sommerville Dance Contest that was held once a month at the school gym. First prize was two hundred dollars. Not much, but it gave the local kids something to do. It certainly kept my two busy.

I looked at the clock on my night stand. Nine-thirty AM. I turned and saw my husband, Ralph snoring peacefully beside me, undisturbed by "Earth Wind and Fire's" steady beat.

After nearly twenty years of marriage, I was still amazed at how he could sleep through practically anything. Let's see, he slept through Jeff's diaper rash, Sylvia's colic, and my post natal blues. I was really in bad shape after Sylvia was born. It didn't bother good old Ralph though. Slept right through the whole time like a baby.

By this time, the music was beginning to get on my nerves, and I felt like slapping Ralph. How could he sleep with that racket going on. Even more annoying, was the fact that he had a stupid blank expression on his face. As if he didn't have a care in the world.

I tumbled out of bed, walked over to the door and yelled, "Can you two give me a break? Have a little consideration. Your father's trying to sleep in here."

As I returned to the bed, I heard the stereo click off. I sat down on the edge of the bed, and fumbled around for my slippers. Of course one of them was under the bed, in the middle, where I couldn't reach it. Oh, the heck with it. I kicked the other slipper off of my foot. It flipped over my head and landed on Ralph's stomach. That's where it stayed. Up ... Down ... Up ... Down, to the rhythm of his steady breathing.

I couldn't stand it any more. I practically ran into the bathroom. I turned the shower on full force and tried to calm down.

While I showered, I came to the conclusion that I hated my entire family. Ralph, Jeff, Sylvia and any children Jeff or Sylvia might have in the future. Twenty years of my life, shot to hell. I'd heard of teen-age runaways, but I wondered how the world would accept a "not quite" middle aged run away.

I was happily toying with the run away idea, when I heard someone come into the bathroom. It was Ralph. Privacy was one of the luxuries that I'd given up twenty years ago when I said, "I do!"

Ralph peeped around the shower curtain. "Good morning beautiful."

I felt like shoving my foot down his throat. Instead I just snatched the shower curtain closed, and bit my lower lip to keep from screaming. I didn't even return his greeting.

After I'd showered and dressed, I headed for the kitchen to fix breakfast. Before I reached the kitchen door, Jeff popped out from nowhere. "Hi, Mom."

I mumbled a "good morning" and brushed pass him.

He seemed to be taking a long time to fill out. At seventeen, I'd expected him to have at least matured a little. Only, he was awkward, too tall for his scrawny frame, and his hands and feet were far too big. Maybe something was wrong with him. Some defect that we neglected to notice. I tried to think back to when he was born. I couldn't think. Well, it's too late now anyway. The damage was done. Just look at him.

Ralph and Sylvia were bumping around the kitchen preparing breakfast. They were so cheerful and happy it was disgusting. So, I just sat down and waited.

What Jeff lacked in physical maturity, Sylvia made up for triple fold. I don't remember ever looking like that, especially at fifteen. She must take after Ralph's family. They all have the tendency for overweight. In fact, he has two sisters who are down right fat. I should have taken this into consideration before I agreed to marry him. I definitely should not have had children by him.

Jeff flopped down in the chair next to me, gawking at the food. He'd eat us out of house and home if we let him have his way.

Everyone was so cheerful. Making unnecessary conversation, trying to include me. Couldn't they see that I didn't want to be included. Couldn't they see that they were all getting on my nerves. Ralph acting like a chef, flipping pancakes like a fool. I wished he'd have dropped them on his stupid head.

Sylvia was bouncing around the kitchen, opening and closing the refrigerator door for one thing or another. I was surprised that she didn't catch one of those big boobs of hers inside. When did all that happen anyway? One minute she was a normal little girl. The next minute she was "Boom-Boom Bubbles" from the Kit Kat Club. And Jeff! I couldn't even stand to look at him. He was just plain silly looking. Even his laugh annoyed me. Lately he seemed to laugh at everything. Maybe he is slightly retarded. Well, if he is, that's from Ralph's side of the family too.

Breakfast was a disaster for me. Nobody paid much attention to my misery. What did I expect anyway? I was living with a bunch of misfits. I was the only normal one in the house.

I had to get out of here. Even if it were just for an afternoon. I'd given up on the run away idea. This group was definitely in sad shape. But, I felt responsible for them. We all have our loads to carry. This family is probably punishment for something I'd done a long time ago.

After breakfast, they wouldn't let me do the dishes. Even that irked me. What were they trying to do? Make me feel guilty? Well, I didn't feel guilty. I felt sick and tired. Sick and tired of them. Sick and tired of my house. And sick and tired of my life. The whole kit and caboodle.

I went out. At first, I didn't know where I was going. I just got on the bus and rode down town. I went into a few stores, but I really didn't feel like shopping. So, I went to a luncheonette and ordered an ice cream sundae. That was the best idea I'd had in a long time. I really enjoyed that sundae. I know it sounds silly, but sitting there, eating my ice cream and watching the people made me feel like a girl again. I used to go to a luncheonette just like this one when I was young. I'd sit there and listen to the music from the juke box and watch the other kids dancing and playing around. In fact, that's where I met Ralph. He asked if he could share my booth with me. I should have known that he had a problem then. Why wasn't he dancing and playing around with the other normal kids?

I was walking down the street, trying to figure out what else I could do to delay going home, when I saw a girl I'd gone to school with. Cynthia Thompson. I called out to her just as she turned the corner. She didn't hear me. I saw her enter the "Manhattan Club", one of our more exclusive places. I checked the money I had in my wallet and debated whether or not to go in.

Inside the Manhattan Club, I had to adjust my eyes to the dim light. I looked around until I caught sight of Cynthia sitting at the bar. Good. She was alone. As I approached, I couldn't help noticing how well dressed she was. I felt shabby in comparison.

"Cynthia, Cynthia Thompson!" I called to her.

She turned, and her expression changed from bewilderment to recognition.

"Gladys Rogers! What a surprise to see you here. How the hell are you anyway?"

"Well, for one thing, it's not Gladys Rogers anymore. I'm married. My name is Shaffer now." I corrected her.

Her eyes looked toward the ceiling, as if she were pondering over something. "Shaffer? Shaffer? Don't tell me you're married to that good-looking Ralph Shaffer?"

Her words caught me off guard.

"Why, yes, Ralph is my husband." I said, and added, "We have two children."

Cynthia looked at me hard for a moment. Her eyes moved up and down. Then she said in almost a whisper. "Well, the little Mole finally grew up."

I cringed at the sound of my old nick name. It took me years to realize that the name had nothing to do with my looks. I was very shy as a youngster, so the kids nick named me "Mole". They said that all I needed was a little hole and I could hide inside forever. I didn't like being reminded of that part of my young years. I didn't remember Cynthia being so cruel either. I just looked at her.

Suddenly, I had nothing at all to say to her. Maybe it wasn't such a good idea to come in here after all.

She looked so cool and confident. She was dressed beautifully. She looked as young as I remembered her in school. I tried to find something wrong with her, to get back at her for bringing back bad memories. But, she was beautiful. She was flawless. I was hurt and miserable.

Then Cynthia began chattering away, unaware of my discomfort. Soon, I was caught up in her conversation. I felt relaxed again.

To hear her tell it, I'd gotten the pick of the litter. I didn't know that Ralph was so popular. Especially with the crowd that Cynthia hung around with. You know, the In-Crowd. The best athletes, the most beautiful girls, the whole bit.

I found out that Cynthia had married her high school sweetheart, Mitchell Groves. They had a son, who is about my Jeff's age. It seems that Mitchell drank a lot and couldn't hold on to a decent job. Cynthia divorced him after two and a half years. I felt very sad for her, but she chattered away. Her failed marriage and divorce were quite normal to her. I guess it has to be. Besides in this day and age, that is normal. I must admit though, that Ralph, with all his faults, has spared me a lot of the ugliness in life.

I touched Cynthia's hand and said, "You know Cynthia, I sympathize with you. It must be very hard on you, trying to raise your son alone."

"Look, Little Miss Muffet, you don't have to feel sorry for me. Besides, I'm not raising my kid alone. I got married again, and I'm not doing too bad for myself either." Her mood changed from chatty to hostile.

7

I couldn't understand why she was so touchy. I decided to just listen and not comment. By this time, I was beginning to miss being home, where people treated me like a person.

I listened as Cynthia told me how she met her present husband. He's a little older than she, but he was already established in business when they met. That explained the expensive way she was dressed.

The Tom Collins I had ordered when I first sat down at the bar was still sitting in front of me half finished. I noticed that Cynthia had downed three of whatever she was drinking and had ordered a fourth. She kept talking.

Her fourth Scotch on the Rocks arrived unceremoniously. She explained that her son had gotten into trouble with drugs last year. He blamed her for having such a horrible time of it. Accusing her of driving his father to drink., He left home after that, and moved in with his father. She hasn't seen him since. She says that she doesn't care. That she did her best for him and that he just didn't appreciate it. Then in a very quiet voice she said, "He was always a selfish, ungrateful kid anyway." She ordered another drink.

I looked at the clock. It was four-thirty in the afternoon. If she continued to drink at this pace, she'd be drunk before six o'clock. I told her that we'd better leave. Maybe take a walk or something before we went home. She refused, saying that she had an appointment with someone at five. I didn't dare ask who it was. From what I'd gathered, I was quite sure that it wasn't her husband. She admitted that their relationship wasn't doing well at all. She'd practically told me, in so many words that she'd had several affairs while married to him. The more she drank, the more personal information she divulged.

I was getting anxious to leave, but I didn't know how to make my exit gracefully. I looked up to see the bartender looking at her, shaking his head. She *was* sad. I felt sad for her. I wanted to help, but didn't know what to do. We were never really good friends. I was never in her league. I guess I'm still not.

I left Cynthia at the bar. I also left my feelings of anxiety and self pity. I took a good look at myself. For the past week I've been a real witch. I should have my head examined. I have a good life. A workable life for me and I should start working at it instead of complaining.

When I unlocked the front door to my house, the first thing that hit me was the sound of "Earth Wind and Fire' blaring from the den. The kids were practicing their dance routine.

I heard Sylvia say, "Jeff, you have to lead with your left foot on the third beat, or you'll throw me off balance".

He answered, "O.K. but you'll have to make a full turn instead of a half. Let's try it."

When I walked in, they both stopped dead in their tracks. I must have been like a crazy person this morning, because they both just stood there looking at me. They didn't know whether to run or turn the stereo off or what to do.

I broke into the silence, "you'd better get those steps down pat if you expect to win that contest tonight."

They exhaled and continued with their dancing. They were good kids. I was proud of them.

"Where's your father?" I said.

Jeff looked up and smiled. Then he pointed toward the bedroom. Just as I thought, Ralph was sprawled across our bed. Only this time he wasn't snoring. I closed the door behind me, sat down on the bed and just looked at him. He *was* handsome. Funny, I couldn't remember the last time that I really looked at him. I could see now why the girls were after him in school. I would be eternally grateful for whatever it was that attracted him to me. I did get a prize, in more ways than one.

I tried to get up without waking him. Suddenly, he reached for me playfully. So, he wasn't asleep after all. No wonder he wasn't snoring.

"And why are you sitting here staring at me? Are you planning to bump me off or something?" He quizzed.

I looked into his eyes for a long moment, then I gave him a kiss with all the tenderness I was feeling at that moment.

"Why would I want to do that? Don't you know that you mean everything to me? By the way, have I thanked you lately for my wonderful life? I love you Darling."

Ralph didn't need any more encouragement. He whispered, "I love you too, Beautiful", and pulled me closer to him. I was glad that I had closed the bedroom door. We wouldn't want to disturb the children.

The End

2

Beyond The Dream

Spring was in the air. Warm breezes stirred provocatively as the last traces of Winter surrendered itself to the subtle charms of the new season's bold declaration. It's presence ever mounting. The change that began as quietly as the melting snow, as gentle as the falling rain, as awesome as a budding flower. Discretely nudging its way onward, until reaching its full potential, its full power, its full bloom.

"Yes, Spring was definitely in the air", Mona thought as the balmy night engulfed her with its sights and sounds. Her heartbeat quickened as she braced herself in the seat of the taxicab that carried her toward her destination.

Through the clear glass windows, she watched as the nights darkness transformed the city streets into a make believe paradise, masqueraded by the bright lights and flashing neon signs. She marveled at the complexities of this flawless transformation.

With sheer determination, Mona fought to block out the apprehensions that plagued her. There was no turning back now. No stopping. For Mona knew that before this night reached tomorrow's dawn, she will have taken for herself a lover. This thought caused a cold chill to engulf her body.

"How did I talk myself into such a hair-brained idea", she mused, as she focused her attention on her immediate surroundings. Cloaking herself within the walls of the moving vehicle, and allowing the engines monotonous hum to lull her quietly back to her resolve.

Leaning against the softly cushioned leather seat, Mona retraced the events that led her to this insane course of action. Insane? The word hung suspended in her mind. Mona knew with all her heart that this journey, this insane gesture, offered the only hope of holding on to the remaining shreds of sanity that she felt seeping rapidly from her grasp these months since her divorce from Howard.

Mona's mind drifted to thoughts of Howard. Howard, her loving husband of fifteen years. Her friend, her love, her life. Howard the miracle worker who patiently turned a shy, puritanical nineteen year old girl into a woman. A woman capable of enjoying unashamedly the thrill of pleasing a man to unbounded heights of ecstasy. Her Howard had awakened within her the searing fires that before laid dormant. Howard, the planter of seed, that when harvested, brought her into the full bloom of motherhood. Howard, only Howard.

"Well, it's all over kiddo, so you'd better make the best of the life you have left." Mona felt the back of her eyes clouding up, and pushed back the slight trickle with the heel of her hand. A grim smile touched her lips as she remembered how only he had this effect on her. Never once during the entire fifteen years of marriage, did her eyes or thoughts stray.

Mona sensed that things weren't right between them for some time, but she hoped with all her heart that somehow she could salvage their strained relationship. Given time, she thought, things would work themselves out.

"What had happened? Where had she gone wrong?" Mona was still searching for answers. She questioned herself constantly. Just when was her love for him replaced by complacency? For it was this last realization that shocked Mona into grievous discernment. Only, it was too late. Too late to salvage their marriage. Even a cordial working arrangement was out of the question.

Although, Howard and Mona were not compatible as mates, their attraction for each other physically still blazed with the passion of youth. They both were very much aware of the fact that this physical bond was not enough to see them through longer years as marriage partners. Mona's problem was that she believed that she could never reach the sensual heights that she reached with Howard.

Mona closed her eyes as she recalled an incident during a time long ago when she and Howard were still very much in love. It was early morning. Dark shadows of the night before fought to maintain their dominance. A dusky hue streaked with hints of sunlight enhanced the prevailing mood.

Mona and Howard lay together peacefully after a night of blissful lovemaking. His passions spent, Howard peered lazily into Mona's eyes and declared arrogantly,

"Woman, I do believe that I've created a monster."

He chuckled softly. Mona felt the slight rumble that shook his body as she reveled in the warmth of his arms that encircled her. He continued, his voice slightly above a whisper,

"Many more nights like last, and I'll be a goner for sure."

13

He tightened his arm around her waist, pressing her closer to him as his other hand toyed with the tips of her small plump breasts.

"You're a lusty little piece, you know that?"

Then almost as if to himself he sighed,

"But, what a way to go."

Mona turned slowly to meet his gaze. This almost provocative movement was heightened by their nakedness. Mona felt Howard's hand drift from the small of her back to a lower position, making tiny circles that tingled her already enflamed skin. When his hand reached its destination, Howard pulled her closer still and pressed her between his hard muscular thighs. Awakened by the newly aroused fires that burned in his loins, he caressed her with a growing urgency. Mounting passions now directed his movements, until finally with a low groan, he rolled over so that he was positioned just above her, only to find her hands pressed firmly against his pounding chest.

Mona stared up at Howard in mock concern.

"Maybe, you're right", she teased.

"You'd better rest a while. After all, I wouldn't want to become a widow before my time."

Pretending to give the matter much thought, she said,

"I know. I'll just find myself a part time lover to help you out. O.K?"

Howard's reply struck Mona with the truth of its words. His passion intensified its meaning. As he held her pinned beneath him, his face so close to hers, that she felt his hot breath.

He spoke in a confident tone.

"I know you well enough my love, to dismiss that fear. You're mine. I awakened your desires and I'm the only one who can satisfy you completely."

Mona was for an instant irritated by his smug attitude. She searched her mind for a flip reply to his statement, but all was forgotten when she felt the hardness of him stir as he plunged deep within her. Her senses were staggered, blocking out all else. There was nothing else, just this moment shared.

Only now as Mona neared her journeys end in the taxicab that had comfortingly become her haven for revelry into private memories, did Howard's words drift back to taunt her with their naked truth.

She truly believed his words and did not think herself capable of loving another man as completely as she did Howard. Mona hated herself for being this way, but these past months of loneliness made it quite clear to her, that she had to make the best of the situation. Months of celibacy has a way of bringing one into a compromising position. Mona was at this point. The point of no return, so to speak.

Here she was, divorced. The product of a failed marriage. Even her son, Keith, was no consolation to her. For at fourteen, he was busy with his own life. Very busy indeed. Sports, the guys, girls and partying. All the things that young people his age are so heavily into. Mona was grateful that his grades were up to par. He was a good son. Mona was very proud of the way he handled himself concerning his parents divorce. In fact Mona was the only one who was thrown completely for a loop.

Exactly one week ago, Mona came to her decision. She intended to rejoin the world of the living. No more sitting at home alone reading or watching television. Not that she didn't enjoy reading or television, it was just the alone part that she couldn't stand any longer. She craved adult conversation, male companionship and of late the need for the more intimate advantages of such a relationship.

"Here we are lady!"

The gruff voice of the cab driver broke into her thoughts. Mona looked around with an uncertain smile.

"Ho-How much?"

The driver tossed an impatient nod towards the meter.

"four dollars even, Ma'am".

Mona fished around in her purse, found her wallet, extracted a five dollar bill and handed it to the driver, indicating for him to keep the change.

Once on the sidewalk, Mona heard the taxicab door close behind her. It sped away, she watched it fade into the night. The taillights mingled with the distant lights of the city, until everything gradually became just a blur to her eyes.

Mona felt a pang of panic that she quickly dismissed in order to familiarize herself with her new surroundings. The neon lights that beckoned from every entranceway took on an enticing glow. Mona made her way towards the door with the brightly lit marquee that read,

"The Passion Flower Discotheque."

Sights, sounds and smells of this new scene filled her. Loud pulsating music filtered through the doorway.

Mona was like a hungry sponge, soaking up the atmosphere. With each step, Mona gained a little more confidence.

"It's been a long time old girl."

Mona reached the door of the Passion Flower. She took a second to contemplate her situation. Realizing the harsh fact that, here she was, a mature single woman, struggling for survival in a young, coupled off world. Matching her passé standards of morality to those of this Uni-Sex, Do your own thing, Self Preservationist existence of this Now generation. Although, Mona did not go along with all or even understand this new scene, she knew that she couldn't let this stop her from living her life to it's fullest potential. She gleaned strength from a saying that came to her from her past.

"I may not play in Count Basie's Band, but I can still dance to his music."

The decision was made. Mona was prepared to dance to the music. What she didn't know was that this decision was just the beginning. The beginning of a chain of events to be etched in her memory, to burn there vividly forever.

Mona entered the Passion Flower Discotheque.

The End

3

Challenge Lost

He's gone now, out of our lives. But, somehow, I expect to see him popping up at any moment or to hear the phone ring, knowing it's him on the other end asking to speak with Cori, my fourteen year old daughter.

How greatly our lives have changed since Gary Thomas came on the scene. Although, he is just shy of eighteen in years, he is old, aged by some pre-mature measure of time. Time that's been quickened by experience and the struggle to survive. "Street wise and city slick" are the terms that come to mind. Only now, knowing what I know about Gary, is more than enough to render these terms inadequate. Gary is more than just city slick, more than just street wise, he was out of a different page from what I have been accustomed to in my lifetime.

I remember the first time I ever saw him, just six short months ago. Months that seem like ages.

He was standing in front of my apartment building. His hands were plunged deep inside the pockets of his gray wool jacket. I couldn't see his face clearly because his collar was pulled high in an attempt to shield his ears from the December chill. The visor of his black cap hooded his eyes.

Without a doubt though, I knew immediately who this young man was. Although knowing who he was didn't bother me at all. What did bother me was his actual presence. What the hell was he doing here ... talking to Cori? Hadn't I just days ago given her explicit instructions to leave this "Gary" character alone? Surely her memory couldn't be that bad.

It was only two days ago that she'd come home from school bursting with news.

"Mom, guess what?" she'd said, whisking pass me, dropping her books down on the table and opening the refrigerator door in one swift motion.

"What?" I responded, bracing myself for the usual "Who did this today in the cafeteria or what happened when so-in-so bugged out on the bus", type of answer.

"There's this new kid that started school today." she replied in her Melba Toliver, news flash of the day voice.

"Oh?"

I wasn't impressed, but she didn't seem to notice.

"Yeah! His name is Gary and he's from New York," she continued.

By this time, she'd succeeded in pulling out all the fixings for her afternoon snack, which consisted of, sandwich, milk, cookies and or chips. No wonder she was hardly ever hungry at dinner time.

"From New York, Huh?"

I chided, holding up my end of the conversation.

20

"Does he seem like a nice boy?"

After what seemed to me, a much too long of a pause, Cori answered with a "wel-l-l!" that trailed off into a little whining noise.

Now, I was curious.

"What's wrong with him?"

"Nothing!" she answered quickly. Too quickly.

Another pause, then "Really Mom, nothing's actually wrong with him."

"Something must be the matter. What does he look like?"

I watched her as she chomped on her sandwich and tried to make a mental note of this *new kid*.

"He's ... all right." She finally said.

"All right? What does that mean, all right?" I probed.

"It means, he looks all right I guess, but ..."

Here it comes, I thought. This kid must have an oversized head or something. Maybe, his nose isn't in the middle of his face where it's supposed to be.

"But what?" I couldn't stand the suspense.

"But, he wore this hat ... a skull cap ..." She took another bite from her sandwich.

"That's it?" He wore a skull cap?"

I just looked at Cori. Here I expected her to tell me of some horrible disfigurement this new kid had and she comes up with "he wore a skull cap."

She was looking straight ahead as if picturing Gary in her mind.

She began to speak,

"He had his hair in an Afro." She took a swallow of milk and continued, It stuck out from the sides of his hat and the hat was just sitting on top of his head ... in a peak." Cori gestured with her hand. A smile tilted the sides of her mouth as she described Gary.

"He really looked funny, Mom ... really funny!"

Well, he didn't sound funny to me. He sounded pretty weird. The kind of boy who would do anything to gain attention.

"... And he was talking to all the girls." Cori giggled. "Acting like he was so-o-o-o cool and everything. Bragging about New York. He thinks he's a real ladies man and that all the girls are going to fall for his *rap*. Honestly, Mom, you should have heard him."

Cori chuckled again. I didn't say anything for a few moments. Then I spoke up.

"Did he say anything to you Cori?"

She looked at me and smiled.

"Yeah, he said something to me. I told you he was talking to all the girls."

Cori has an irritating way of trying to evade giving me direct answers when it suits her to do so.

"What did he say to you Cori?" I prodded.

"Huh?" she quipped. Knowing full well what I meant.

"What - did - this - new - boy - say - to - you - Cori?"

I enunciated each syllable so there would be no further pretense at not understanding my meaning. I felt very much the interrogator, but I didn't care. I wanted to know.

"Well?" I persisted.

There was no way for her to get out of answering me now.

She gulped, "He said, Hello sweetheart, how are you today?"

I tried to picture a person who obviously looked strange and chose to do so, talking to my daughter. Visions of Bozo the Clown or the Banana Man or worse glued themselves to my consciousness. Imaging, Bozo the Clown "rapping" to my little girl and trying to sound so grown up.

" And just how old is this boy?" I wanted to know.

"Seventeen."

That did it. Seventeen? Why he was practically a man. And my goodness, if he didn't have better sense than to run around looking weird and rapping to innocent little girls, well, there was just no hope for him.

It was at this point in our conversation of two days ago that I expressly forbade Cori to have anything whatsoever to do with this boy. Issue closed. That was that.

Now, here he was, bold as brass and then some, in front of my house, talking with Cori.

It was a Saturday and I had worked my usual Saturday shift. I had stopped for a few groceries on my way home and was tired and not in too good a mood. The car fitted nicely into the parking space in front of my building. Cori saw me as I drove up. She was nervous. Her eyes shifted from the boy standing next to her to the direction of the car to the boy again and back to the car before she decided to wave to me. He did nothing, although he knew I was there.

When I got out of the car, I called to them, "Come help me with these things." Meaning the bags of groceries.

Cori ran to the car to help. *He* did nothing. Just as I thought, no home training. This kid doesn't even have consideration enough for Cori to try to impress her mother. Too hip and citified to help with grocery bags, I guessed. I knew I wasn't going to like this boy, I just knew it.

As Cori gathered one of the bags into her arms, she gushed, "He just came over, Mom, ... What could I do? ... I knew you'd be mad, so I didn't invite him upstairs. I told him he had to stay downstairs because I wasn't allowed company when my mother isn't home ... Mom, are you mad? ... What could I do?"

Poor kid, she was in the middle. She didn't know what to expect. Actually I didn't know what to expect either, but Cori didn't know that. I hated to make her suffer, so I told her that she'd done the right thing by not inviting Gary inside the house.

She walked in front of me carrying the grocery bag and trying with all her might to appear natural. Her efforts didn't work. She stumbled and almost dropped the bag. *Mr. Hip-de-dip* stood watching from the steps, offering still no assistance.

Her eyes pleaded as she said, "Mom, this is Gary, Gary Thomas, the new boy I told you about."

"I know." was my reply. "Hello Gary."

"Gary, this is my mother", Cori continued unnecessarily.

"I know", said Gary, a hint of defiance in his voice. "Hi, Mrs. Adams."

The first thing I noticed about Gary Thomas were his dark piercing eyes that stared directly into my own. Bold and challenging.

I smiled my *warm friendly, nice to meet 'cha* smile. He continued to stare unchanged in his expression.

Cori shifted from one foot to the other.

"What are you, too cool to smile?" I said, not caring that I sounded hostile. I was.

"There's nothing to smile about." he answered matter of matter-of-factly.

He was right of course. There wasn't a single thing in the world to smile about at that moment. Only now my face was frozen into this fake smile that felt pasted on like a hideous grin. I knew I looked foolish. I also knew that this young man was not very hard to dislike. An understatement. I hated him.

Turning toward the door, and with a lack of anything better to say I invited him upstairs.

"Would you like to come inside ... out of the cold?"

Cori led the way. Gary was second and I trailed behind, carrying the other packages.

"Hi Mom!"

I was greeted at the head of the stairs by my younger daughter, Carol.

"Oh? You already met Gary?" She started, then after glancing in Cori's direction, she decided not to continue. Somehow I got the impression that there was a conspiracy going on ... against me.

My feelings of hostility changed to paranoia.

"Come help me in the kitchen, Carol, I said trying to sound light. Cori, ask Gary to have a seat ... maybe he'd like a soda or chips or cookies or something."

This took all the effort I could scrape together. Lord knows I felt anything but hospitable towards this young man. He was an annoyance, an intruder, a threat.

Why in heavens name should I be threatened by Gary's presence? After all, he was nothing but a *pip-squeak kid*, right?

Carol and I busied ourselves in the kitchen. I heard mumbling from the living room. Cori and Gary were talking. His voice sounded so deep. If I didn't know better, I'd swear there was a man in there.

Cori giggled. I dropped a fork in the sink startling Carol. She looked at me questioningly.

"So, what's wrong with you?" I snapped, "I just dropped a fork, that's all."

Her silence made me even more edgy.

"Well?" I hissed.

"Nothing ... nothing's wrong with me Mom," she said, lowering her eyes.

Now I felt bad. I shouldn't have yelled.

"Hey listen, I said, after we finish up in here, you want to play a game of cards?" I gave her a little hug, hoping she'd forgive me for being such a grouch. She did, and all was well again. Carol was still at that *nice* age, child like and manageable. So much easier to deal with than Cori. What a difference two years can make. Cori didn't know whether she wanted to be a little girl or a woman. And her varying moods were about to send me to the *Loony Bin*. I just couldn't do anything right anymore. When I tried treating her as I would a young lady, she was very much the little girl. When I knew for sure that she was my little Cori, she turned into Miss Cori Leigh Adams, woman of the world. Six in one hand, half dozen in the other. I just couldn't win.

We did play cards. All of us, Cori, Gary, Carol and myself. At least that was one way of keeping my eye on things without being too obvious. Or, so I thought. I didn't trust Gary and he knew it. In fact, I think he was amused by my discomfort. Every time I looked up from my cards, I was met by Gary's gaze. Victory in his eyes. The prize, My Cori. Also, I didn't like the way he looked at Cori. Not the way a little boy looks at a little girl, but the way a man looks at a woman. I couldn't stand it.

In the few short hours of our first meeting, Gary managed to establish his presence and to challenge me for my precious little girl. Needless to say, he won the challenge.

Although my Cori is still my little girl, *sometimes*. I can't help but notice the subtle difference in her demeanor. A maturity that was bound to happen one day. A maturity that I wasn't quite ready for.

I call this maturing of Cori the *Gary Experience*. This time for me was filled with worry and concern. I didn't want Cori to get hurt or damaged. I also knew she had her own dilemmas during this period.

With all my apprehensions, I think she handled herself well. Only, I'm still a bit of a wreck. And to think, I have to go through this again with Carol. Oh Well!

Yes, Gary is gone from our lives now, and I'm happy to say that for me the memory of him grows dimmer with each passing day. Life must go on.

The End

4

Chances Are

It's 3:00 am. The all night food market is empty except for the night crew and two shoppers.

Vivian Grant is shopping at this ridiculous hour because she can't sleep.

Lester McKnight chose this market because it was the only place he knew that would be open at this hour of the morning.

Both Vivian and Lester are recovering from love affairs that have ended abruptly.

Two days ago, Charlie, Vivian's live in gay lover decided that their arrangement wasn't working out. As a matter of fact, Charlie decided to get married to a man no less. It was hard for Vivian to accept this change of heart. Vivian was confused. Charlie split, leaving Vivian quite broken hearted and hurt.

Lester on the other hand just got the boot. About an hour and a half ago, Dana, the love of Lester's life, informed him that his presence was no longer needed nor desired. Since the apartment was in Dana's name, Lester didn't argue the point. Also, *"King-Kong"* Dana's new fellow made Lester's decision a simple one. He gathered his few belongings and left.

So, here they are, Vivian and Lester, two wee-hour of the morning shoppers.

Lester: I'd get this brand if I were you.

Vivian: Excuse me.   Were you talking to me? (ridiculous question. no one else was within earshot)

Lester: I said, (pointing to the can of beets he's holding), This brand is much better. Less salt.

Vivian: Oh! (returns the can she is holding to it's place on the shelf)

Lester: Here! (tosses the can to her)

Vivian: (catches the can and looks at it) This isn't the same.

Lester: I know. I told you, it's much better. Less salt. Remember?

Vivian: This is a can of peas. I was buying a can of beets ... See? (throws the can of peas back to him)

Lester: (catches the can of peas) Oh yeah. (returns the can of peas to the shelf)

Vivian turns her shopping cart and walks quickly down the aisle. Trying to get away from Lester. Lester runs behind her.

Lester: Hey wait a minute. You forgot your beets.

Vivian: (turns abruptly)   Look!   You'd better stop
            following me, or ... or ... there's going to be
            trouble. **Big** trouble.

Lester: Yeah, ok. (turns and walks away from Vivian)

Vivian glares at Lester as he walks down the aisle away
from her. She is surprised that she was able to get rid of
him as easily as she did.

Vivian returns to her shopping. Every now and then she
spots Lester, standing at the end of an aisle, peering into the
frozen food case, reading the back of a cereal box, but not
actually picking up anything. In fact, Lester doesn't even
have a shopping cart.

She watches him. She is curious but leery. He must be
some kind of nut, Vivian concludes. Who else but a nut
would hang around an all night market at 3:00 in the
morning? She'd better keep one eye on him at all times.

After finishing her marketing, Vivian looks for Lester at the
check-out counter but does not see him.   Good, she
thought, maybe he left the market and went back to the
Funny Farm where he obviously belongs.

Once outside the market, with packages in her arms, Vivian
heads for her car that's parked in the parking lot. Suddenly,
she feels a blow to the middle of her back and is knocked
down. Her packages go flying in every direction and
someone is tugging at her purse. With one last violent yank
the thief frees her purse and runs into the darkness.

Vivian begins screaming.

Vivian: My bag! My bag. He took my bag.

By this time, the supermarket people are all outside the store gathering around Vivian. One of them helps Vivian to her feet just in time for her to spot Lester limping towards them carrying Vivian's pocketbook.

Vivian: That's him! That's him! Someone call the police ... Arrest that man. He attacked me and stole my pocketbook.

Supermarket Person: Calm down lady. Looks to me like he's bringing your pocketbook back to you.

Vivian: He's crazy I tell you. Where's the police? I want to press charges.

Lester: Here, take this Buddy. (handing the purse to the Supermarket Person) I'm getting out of here ... (to Vivian) You're sick. You're really sick, you know that?

By this time two police officers arrive.

Policeman: O.K., What seems to be the problem here?

Vivian: Arrest that man (points to Lester) He hit me and snatched my pocketbook.

Lester: Now, wait a minute. I just tried to help her officer, that's all.

Policeman: You want to tell me exactly what happened?

Vivian: Yeah, go ahead. Try to get out of it. (smugly)

Lester: I see her come out of the store. Then this guy, a young kid about 15 or 16, comes out of no where, pushes her, grabs her bag and takes off down the street. I run after him about a block and a half. He stumbles, drops the bag, I snatch it ... but he manages to kick me, I double over, hit the ground with my face, because I'm holding on to her pocketbook with my hands and couldn't brace myself, then the kid runs away and I bring her bag back to her and ... well, that's it ...Except now, she's trying to accuse me of ...

Vivian: Don't believe him officer. He's lying. He did it! He did it!

Policeman: Did anybody else see what happened here?

Supermarket Person: All I know is I hear her screaming her lungs out. When I get out here, this guy (points to Lester) is hobbling over here trying to give her back her pocketbook.

Policeman: (after viewing the situation) I think you got it all wrong Miss. This man is only trying to help you. You see. He got your pocketbook back for you ...(looks harder at Vivian) Now Miss, .. If he were a thief, why would he bring your pocketbook back. ... That wouldn't make sense now would it?

Vivian: But, he's crazy!! Who knows why crazy people do the things that they do?

Everyone looks at Vivian as if **she's** nuts. She realizes how silly her accusation is.

Vivian: Well ... He could be crazy.

Policeman: There now. Seems to me, you should be thanking this man instead of trying to get him arrested.

Lester: Forget it!

Vivian began picking up her groceries. The Supermarket people go back inside the store.

Policeman: I'll have to take your names and addresses. Then we'll cruise the area and get back to you if we find anything.

Vivian: Vivian Grant, 404 North Aldine 921-7772. (she continues to pick up her groceries)

Lester: Lester McKnight, 2404 Bower Drive, 927-4826.

The officers get into the police car. Vivian, carrying her packages, walks to her car. She sees Lester limping down the street slowly. She hesitates, then ...

Vivian: Hey! ... Hey you! ... Lester McKnight! (Lester stops, turns around and looks at Vivian) ...Are you OK? ... I mean ...

Lester: N-o-o-o, I'm not all right! My face hurts ... and so does my pride.

Vivian: I'm sorry.

Lester: Yeah, I'll bet. (starts walking again)

Vivian: Hey! Hey! Wait a minute. (Lester stops)
           I ... I ... just want to say ... Thank you ...

Lester: Ah..hum..ph (starts walking away again)

Vivian: Hey! Wait a min ...

Lester: (turning abruptly)
           Look, you'd better stop following me or there's
           going to be trouble ... **Big** trouble!

Vivian and Lester look at each other. Then they both start
to laugh.

Vivian: I deserved that.

Lester: Yes, you did.

Vivian: Can I offer you a lift home?

Lester: No, but you can offer me a cup of coffee.

Vivian: Huh?

Lester: Coffee .. a cup of coffee. You **do** know how to
           make coffee don't you?

Vivian: Yes, I know how to make coffee.

Lester: Good! (takes the packages from Vivian)
           That **is** your car over there, isn't it. (leading her
           to the car)

Vivian: Yes, that's my car. (allowing him to lead her to
            the car)

So, Vivian and Lester meet!

Vivian walks to her car thinking how nice it's going to be to
have someone to share breakfast with again. She's looking
forward to Lester's company and maybe his friendship.

Lester on the other hand has a nagging doubt about this
new encounter becoming a real friendship. Although, he
would desperately like for this relationship to develop, he is
afraid that once Vivian discovers his *secret*, she'll feel
misled and deceived, making friendship impossible.

Lester knows that he has to tell her his *secret*. That his last
lover Dana, is a man and that he is gay! Lester hopes that
Vivian will understand.

Of course she will!!!!!!!!

The End

5

Farewell My Tears

Another Friday night. Edna watched silently as Dwayne dressed for his regular night out with the boys. Only for the past few years, she knew that these nights out were not necessarily with the boys. A little hint here, a slip of the tongue there, leaving very little room for doubt. Edna had given up arguing. Anyway, arguing never accomplished anything but a very uncomfortable Sunday. And who needs that?

Through it all, dutiful Edna endured. She'd put up with this vain, conceited, selfish man for most of her adult life.

When things first started to fall apart, Edna used to tell herself that the twins Craig and Carol needed their father. What a joke. Dwayne was never much of a family man. He was never much of anything come to think of it. Always making excused for his failures. His favorites were "The System" and "A Black Man sees a hard way to go." Oh yes, and of course there was "Edna." Dwayne always managed to blame Edna for everything that was wrong in his life. In fact, that's why he needed these Friday nights out with the boys. He needed get away from the stress and her nagging. What Dwayne failed to realize was that Edna had stopped *nagging* or even really talking to him about three years ago. He was so busy doing his own thing and thinking that he was getting away with something to notice her withdrawal from their relationship. Dwayne was too narcissistic to act, think or feel anything beyond himself.

Edna was sick of him and sick of his half-assed excuses. As far as she was concerned, he was nothing but a "Sorry Asshole" with nothing to show for twenty years of marriage, but the same five room apartment that they'd started out with.

Now that the kids weren't really kids anymore, Edna was forced to face the cold hard facts of her own life. At age 40, what did she have? Dwayne? A 46 year old, gray behind macho man?

How could this have happened to her. This man used to be her strong handsome Ebony God, her Black Prince. It's tragic how faded dreams and the stark reality of life have a way of separating the Princes from the toads.

Dwayne had just finished shaving. Edna caught him grinning at his reflection in the mirror. Pleased with himself.

Dwayne, Edna thought to herself, you are definitely a **toad**. Beautiful, Black and proud, but a toad none the less.

Well tonight, Buddy-Boy, she mused, I've got a surprise for your "Black Butt."

She watched him admiring himself for a few moments before speaking.

"I'm going with you tonight Dwayne."

The words rolled from her lips with deliberate ease.

"Say What?" Dwayne questioned. Obviously annoyed by her declaration.

"I said that I'm going with you tonight. Craig and Carol are spending the weekend at mommy's again, and I have nothing else to do, so ..."

"Not tonight Edna ... How would that look? ... You'd only be out of place. ... Nah ... we'd better make it some other time."

"O.K. Dwayne ... Just thought I'd ask."

Edna didn't argue. She knew that Dwayne wouldn't want her to go with him anyway. In fact, she'd counted on it.

Edna had made plans of her own. She went into the bathroom and filled the tub with water.

"Hand me that jar of bubble bath, will you Dwayne?"

The water felt warm and tranquil, relieving her body of stress and tension . The aroma of the strawberry scented bubble bath filled her nostrils. Edna rested her head against the back of the tub.

"I'm leaving now, Babe!" Dwayne sounded happy and confident again believing that he'd gotten over yet another time.

His huge frame loomed over the tub. He bent down to kiss her, being very careful not to muss his clothes. Edna fought the urge to splash. The only thing that stopped her was her strong will to live.

Her father and two brothers had conditioned her from childhood to respect the "three don'ts" when living in a Black man's household.

Don't mess with a Black man's clothes! Don't mess with a Black man's car and don't mess with a Black man's money.

The moment of madness passed. Edna didn't splash.

She heard the front door close and lock. Dwayne was gone. Edna found herself once again, at home and alone.

But not for long, she promised herself. Tonight will be different.

After a soothing bath, Edna scanned her closet. She finally decided to wear a red beaded dress that she'd gotten to wear to one of Dwayne's office parties 4 years ago. The dress was mid calf in length and had a scoop neckline. It was simple in design, however Edna's full figure complemented the lines and the red flattered the delicate tones of her caramel colored skin. She looked beautiful. Even more than beautiful, Edna looked sensuous.

"Well, old girl, not bad at all".

Edna smiled at her reflection.

"It's amazing what a little make-up can do".

Her large brown eyes sparkled beneath heavy lashes, accented by the mascara. A hint of plum colored her eyelids. Her cheeks, already rosy with excitement, blended with the pink rose petal blush that highlighted her flawless complexion. Burgundy lip gloss shimmered as a smile teased the corners of her full lips.

An hour later, Dwayne pulled his car into the car port. He got out of the car then reached back in to get the dozen red roses he'd gotten for Edna. He couldn't quite put his finger on it, but he had sensed something in the air and something in Edna's mood which caused him to back out of his usual Friday night fling.

Dwayne entered the house and called for Edna.

In the bedroom, Dwayne found the note neatly pinned to his pillow. He couldn't even bring himself to pick it up. Instead his eyes focused themselves on the words written in Edna's neat handwriting.

Dwayne,

   Don't wait up for me. I've gone out with the girls.

   Edna

Dwayne sank heavily on the bed with the flowers still in his hand. His mind raced. His thoughts traveled the span of the last twenty years in an instant. There was nothing he could do now but wait.

...Out with the girls! ...Out with the girls! Those words seem to echo his every Friday night out with the boys.

The End

6

Grief Belongs to Yesterday

What a day for a funeral!

It should have been raining. Instead, Spring was at her beautiful best. It was early May. The sun was shining and not a single cloud marred the sky. Gentle breezes aroused the air with the scented freshness of floral blossoms. Picture book perfect. The kind of day my mother would have enjoyed.

I hadn't seen my mother in twenty years. Now she was dead and I was here, having a very difficult time trying to connect my proper emotions.

Exactly what I felt as I watched the proceedings, will never be clear to me. Seeing all the familiar faces from my childhood, each one having it's own special significance. Each one bringing back countless memories. Memories that distracted me from the reason I had to return home after all these years.

Someone sobbed loudly. I looked up. It was Sam, a little older perhaps, but sill as good-looking as ever.

Sam was my mother's lover ... and also, the reason I left home so abruptly at the tender age of fifteen.

I had to get away. First of all, it wasn't easy for me to accept the fact that my mother even had a lover, and especially not Sam. Sam, whom I thought was merely a close friend. Sam, who was always there showing concern, helping mom whenever possible. Sam, who was there even before my parents divorced. Good-old Sam. Loyal Sam. Devoted friend Sam ... Sam, who made a pass at me the night I left home. At least that's what I tried to persuade myself into believing actually happened. At the time I was so confused. Fact and fiction were one.

I saw Sam kissing my mother and I thought at first it was all a big joke. Then it hit me. It wasn't a joke at all. Everything became clear to me then. Mom's and Sam's **real** relationship. Everything. I wanted to hurt them the way they had just hurt me. When Sam tried to console me, I felt nothing but hatred for Sam and hatred for my mother.

I couldn't face what I knew to be true. So I escaped within myself, to my own fabrications, holding on to the sanctity of my lie. Using that lie as justification because I couldn't face my mother knowing the truth. I couldn't deal with the fact that she and Sam ... Oh my God! Not with Sam. Sam, short for Samantha!

The End

7

On My Own

I was young. I was restless. I was ready. But, was I ready
to be ... On my own!

It was shortly after I'd turned twenty, that I began to notice
a restlessness within myself that wasn't there before. After
all, I thought to myself, I was young, I was pretty, and I had
my whole life ahead of me. I was ready. Ready for
whatever life had to offer. The time was now, and I had to
make my move. The first thing I had to do, was to tell my
sister that it was time for me to strike out on my own. As I
expected, there was a scene. Sometimes she carried this
big sister act a little bit too far. To hear her tell it, you'd
think I was still a baby.

I'd been living with my sister, Tina and her husband Sam
for the past twelve years, ever since our mother died.
Mom's death was a shock for me. I don't remember her
ever being sick. I just came home from school one day as
usual, and there she was. A heart attack. I never knew my
father, and the only other family I had was Tina and Sam.
So, Tina took over, even though she had two little ones and
a third on the way. I was eight at the time. We became one
big happy family. Tina, at times was a little protective, but
I didn't mind. I knew that this was her way of showing that
she loved me. don't get me wrong, I love Tina too. I love
my whole family, Sam and the kids, but like I said before,
I was twenty, and I was restless. I just had to get away.
So, I let Tina rant and rave about how I was too young to

live alone, and how she'd always planned for me being with her until I got married. That's a laugh. I had no intention of getting married until I had lived a little. And I certainly couldn't do that cooped up here with her and Sam and the kids.

Tina finally calmed down long enough for me to explain the way I felt. She just couldn't understand how I could be so different from herself, and want a life that neither of us knew anything about. I persuaded her to let me move out on a trial basis. With the understanding that if I couldn't handle it, I would come back home. Fat chance.

I gave my two weeks notice. My job as receptionist for the Mayfair Candy Company, had served it's purpose well, but it was time to move on. Everyone came over to my desk that last day to say good-bye. The friends I'd made there over the past three years, got together and bought me a gift. Barbara, the girl I usually ate lunch with was elected to present it to me. We were about the same age, and had started working for Mayfair on the same day. In fact, in the beginning, the other employees used to mix up our names. They'd call me Barbara and they'd call her Irene. We even made a joke about it.

Barbara carried this big box over to my desk. It had a pretty blue bow in the middle of it, with a card attached. I opened the card and read the list of names. When I got to Barbara's name, I saw that she had printed, *a.k.a. Irene*, right next to it. I looked up and saw her brush away a tear. I felt like crying too. We'd had some good times and a lot of laughs. I was really going to miss her.

Inside the box was a beautiful leather travel bag, with my initials engraved on it, "I.M.S.", for Irene Mae Sommers. I wondered how they found out what my middle name was. I never used it.

For the rest of the day we just kidded around. Bob, the office flirt called over to me, "Try not to miss me while you're gone."

I walked over to him, handed him a piece of paper, and said, "Put your name and number on here, just in case I get lonely."

Everyone knows that Bob is happily married and a grandfather. My little joke shut him up good. He just looked at the piece of paper and didn't say anything.

"Hey Irene!"

I turned to see Jim from shipping, grinning from ear to ear. "This place is not going to be the same without you, Babe." He calls everybody "Babe". Then Helen, one of the clerks, said, "Yeah, maybe we should close this dump down, and all of us should take a vacation." A voice from the back room called out, "oh sure, Helen, If they closed this place down, you'd probably die from shock. Your system couldn't take it."

We all got a laugh out of that, because there's a saying at the plant that Helen was there when they built Mayfair. She's the first stone. Needless to say, we didn't get much work done that day, but I was still glad when it was over.

When I got home that night, Sam was sitting at the kitchen table with an envelope in his hand. As usual, Tina was at the stove preparing dinner for us. She looked up from the pot she was stirring and said, "how'd it go today?"

I just shrugged my shoulders, and lifted the box with my travel bag for her to see. She walked over and looked inside and said, "Oh, that's very nice, and it has your initials on it too." She smiled, "Look Sam, at the present that Irene's friends gave her. Isn't it classy? Nothing but the best for my baby sister." She gave me a hug, and told me that dinner would be ready in a few minutes. Tina was pretty, but when she smiled, she was beautiful.

The kids were in the living room looking at television.. Mike and Richie, the two boys were on the floor as usual and Linda sat on the corner of the couch.

"Hi!" was all I got from the boys, but Linda spotted my present, and like most girls, her curiosity got the better of her. She followed me into my room.

"What's in the box, Aunt Irene?" She inquired.

"Oh, it's a present. The people on my job got it for me."

She peered inside, as if she were uncovering a great secret. Before Linda had a chance to comment on the travel bag, we heard Tina's voice calling to us from the kitchen. It was time for dinner.

After we'd eaten, I went right to my room. I finished packing my few things, took a nice hot bath, and relaxed. I couldn't sleep. I was too nervous for sleeping. All I could think about was my trip in the morning. My new life. I'd been in this town in South Jersey long enough. I couldn't wait to try my wings somewhere else.

Even if it were only across the border in New York.

I heard soft tapping on my bedroom door. Tina and Sam were standing in the light from the partially opened door. "Irene, Irene, are you asleep?"

I sat up in bed and motioned for them to come into the room.

"What's up?" I questioned.

Sam spoke first. "Well, you left so fast after dinner that I didn't get a chance to talk to you about your trip tomorrow. Tina and I know that you have a little money saved, but we thought that until you get yourself settled, you could use a little extra help. Its not much, so you'll have to economize for a while."

He stopped speaking and handed me the white envelope that he had earlier. I opened the envelope to find that my sister and brother in-law had given me three thousand dollars. Now, that may not seem like much to a lot of people, but I knew that they didn't have this kind of money to throw around. I tried to tell them that I couldn't take the money, but Tina just waved her hand and told me that this was money that they were saving for me, whenever I decided to get married, or go to college, or whatever. So they figured that my branching out was the whatever or close enough to it.

I just sat there on my bed and stared at the two of them like a complete fool. Sam broke the silence with a nervous cough, and said that he'd better get some sleep, if he were going to get up to take me to the train station in the morning. We said good-night, and after they left, I cried myself to sleep.

I awoke extra early in the morning. I don't know if it was from nervousness or fear of missing my train. I didn't look at Tina, because if I did, I would probably have changed my mind at the last minute and stayed home like she wanted me to do.

We got to the station in just enough time for Sam to give me some last minute instructions. My train pulled in. I boarded. I was on my way at last.

I had visited New York only twice in my entire life. Once when Sam surprised us all with tickets for the circus, and again when Tina and I decided to take Mike, Richie and Linda to see a show at the Radio City Music Hall. It all seemed so different now. I was alone, and on my own. This new feeling of independence made me tingle. I felt happy and alive, and very grown up.

My first stop was at the newspaper stand at the Port Authority. I had to find someplace to stay as soon as possible. Sam had instructed me to stay at a hotel until I found an apartment. With my money situation, I figured that I'd better try to find an apartment right now. So, I found myself a clean little diner, sat down in a booth and began my search.

I was there for about an hour with the same cup of coffee, when the waitress came over to me and asked if there were something else I wanted. I guess I did look kind of peculiar, just sitting there like a bump on a log. I don't even like coffee. I should have ordered something else.

I sensed the waitress growing impatient. I ordered a hamburger and a coke, remembering that I hadn't eaten breakfast.

Finding an apartment wasn't as easy as I thought it would be. The places that sounded good were too expensive. And the ones that I could afford, only offered the barest essentials Another thing that I hadn't anticipated, was my lack of knowledge of the city. I didn't know where to go or how to get there if I did. I was beginning to feel uncomfortable. It must have shown on my face, because when the waitress came back with my food, she smiled at me and said, "Things can't be all that bad, Honey, now can they?"

I wanted to tell her my problem, but decided against it. She might be one of those weirdoes that you hear about in the city. This is another thing that was beginning to creep up on me. Suddenly, I didn't trust anybody. Everyone and everything was a menace to me. Even the little boy that sat at the other end of the diner with his mother, eating French fries, with far too much ketchup. I thought to myself, he's probably some freakish dwarf, getting his kicks pretending to be a kid, with a prostitute acting like his mother. I caught myself staring at the two of them, so I turned my eyes toward the plate that was placed before me.

Staring at my food was not such a good idea. My hamburger looked like a face that you'd see in some horror movie. I could almost swear that it stuck it's tongue out at me.

It didn't take me long to figure out what was happening to me. Unadulterated panic. I couldn't help myself. I felt like running, but I stayed put. I didn't have any place to run to. I closed my eyes and tried not to think. If only I could lie down for a minute. I pushed my hamburger away from me and rested my head on my arms. The roaring in my brain began to subside, but the pounding in my temples was agony. I had a splitting headache. I knew I was going to be sick if I didn't lie down somewhere.

Then, from out of nowhere I heard a voice, "Miss? Is there anything wrong?" Then, I felt someone tapping on my shoulder. That did it. I jumped about three feet in the air, turned and found myself face to face with a complete stranger. I was sure that he was some kind of sex fiend or pervert of some sort. By this time everyone in the diner was looking at me. Everything began to close in.

The diner must have been about two feet in diameter. I had to get out of this place, or these maniacs were going to kill me or hold me prisoner or something else so horrible that I couldn't even imagine.

I heard someone screaming. I was out of the door and half way down the block when I realized that I was the one who was screaming. I couldn't stop running. Suddenly I felt myself being flung to the ground. Imagine, me being tackled on a street by a pervert and an angry mob in the background cheering him on. It was all over for me then. I just couldn't take any more. I vomited, and right before I passed out I heard someone say, "She must be on drugs." I wondered who they were talking about. Then nothing. Total darkness. Peace at last.

When I woke up, my neck ached and my mouth tasted like my tongue had been used to mop the floor of a kennel. I tried to sit up. My head almost fell off. So, I sank back into the softness of the couch that I was lying on and tried to piece my thoughts together. I remembered what had happened, and how I got into this situation. I felt stupid. What on earth had gotten into me. I had to apologize to someone. I only wish I knew who that someone was.

I looked around the room. There was a desk with papers thrown all over. There was what appeared to be a bar in the corner, but I wasn't sure, because my eyes were still a little out of focus. Also, I was in semi-darkness. My eyes searched for a light switch.

The door opened, and a man walked into the little room. I could tell from my glimpse of the other room, exactly where I was. I was in the room in back of the diner that I had tried to flee from a while ago. The man turned on the light. While my eyes were adjusting, I heard him say to me, "You gave us quite a scare, young lady. We didn't know what was wrong with you."

Suddenly, I remembered my three thousand dollars that I had stashed away inside my travel bag. I looked around the room for my belongings. They were almost hidden behind the desk, tucked away neatly in the corner.

"Don't worry Miss, your things are all here. I had them brought here when they carried you back after you tried to run out without paying your tab."

Nothing missing? ... Run out without paying? ... He must be crazy. I wouldn't do anything like that. I tried to defend myself, but I choked on something, and started to cough. The man snapped back at me.

"Look, why don't you clean up a little bit. There's a bathroom through that door to your right. And, I'll be back in a little while, to find out what the hell's going on around here."

Then he just walked out and slammed the door behind him. I got annoyed then. Who did he think he was, treating me as if I were a criminal. I walked over to my things, very carefully. I didn't want to shake my head any more than I had to.

Well, at least my money was still there. And my things were still in tact. I picked out a few clean pieces for myself and went into the bathroom. I was glad that I didn't have to go out into the dining area. I was really a mess.

The bathroom was surprisingly clean. It even had a shower installed. I thought, "This must be somebody's apartment. Maybe the owner of the diner or something like that."

The water felt good, and my headache was going away. I stayed in the shower for about a half hour or so. I almost forgot where I was for a short lived minute. For as soon as I stepped out of the shower, I heard a rap on the bathroom door.

"Who is it?" My voice sounded strange, even to me.

I heard a woman call out to someone in the other room. "She's O.K. Steve." And then to me she yelled, "Hurry it up in there Doll, someone's out here waiting to talk to you."

I started to get nervous again. What if they called the police? What if I have to spend the night in jail, because I don't have any place else to stay? What If they looked through my bags, and called Tina and Sam? I would just die. I couldn't go home now.

Wait a minute. I'm twenty years old. Nobody can force me to do anything that I don't want to do. Bad situations are made to be handled. This was a bad situation, and I was determined to handle it.

I dried myself off as best I could with the paper towels that were there. No one thought to give me a cloth one. I put on the clothes that I'd picked out, and tied my hair back with a scarf. It was still wet. My hair dryer was in my bag in the other room. I wrapped my dirty clothes in a plastic bag, then threw them in the trash can. I didn't want to see those clothes again. I took one last look in the mirror. I looked presentable. My hand reached for the door knob, and I was in the other room facing the same man who had been so rude to me before.

"Are you waiting to speak with me?"

My question must have surprised him, because he stood up a little too quickly, and almost knocked over the glass that was on the table next to the couch. He extended his hand in a gesture for me to join him on the couch.

"No thank you. I'd rather stand if you don't mind".

He looked puzzled, but didn't insist. I was glad for that. He didn't say anything for what seemed like an eternity. I couldn't stand the silence.

"So, what did you want to talk to me about?" As soon as I said that, I realized how idiotic it sounded.

Still, he said nothing. I felt like going up the walls. Instead, I started talking, putting my foot deeper into my mouth.

"Look, I don't know who you are, but you've got what happened this afternoon all backwards. First of all, I was not trying to run out without paying my bill. In fact I'm prepared to settle my account right now, and I'll be leaving here as soon as possible."

He just looked at me, as if he were trying to find a way to break some terrible news to me. But, he said nothing. By this time, my foot was to deep in my mouth that my toes were tickling my tonsils.

"If I've caused you any trouble, I'm sorry. I didn't intend to get sick in your restaurant. But, things like that do happen. So, I'll just get my luggage and pay for whatever damage I've done. Then I'll be on my way."

He looked up then, and I thought I saw him shake his head as if he pitied someone. Boy, I thought to myself, this man is really ready for the loony bin. What in the world was wrong with him. I knew he could talk. I heard him talking a little while ago. Maybe he's throwing a fit or something. He was really annoying me. I had to get myself out of this place, and fast.

I started moving slowly toward my luggage, all the time keeping my eyes focused on him, just in case he tried something weird. Slowly, slowly. I crept. He had his head down. I moved ever so quietly.

Suddenly, he stood up. I almost wet my pants. I stopped dead in my tracks. This nut was actually walking towards me with a strange dumb-butt expression on his face. I prepared myself for the worst. He extended his hand again, in what appeared to be a kind gesture.

"Just calm down Miss. Nothing is all that bad for you to try a dumb stunt like you tried this afternoon. Why, you're young. You have everything to live for. so, why don't you just sit down, and maybe we can get in touch with your family."

He put on a fake patronizing smile and said in a big brother kind of way, "I was just about to have a cup of coffee, would you like a cup?"

I couldn't believe what was happening. This reject from the funny farm thought that I tried to kill myself. That's why he was acting this way. He thought there was something wrong with me and that look of pity was for me.

"O.K. Mister, just hold on a minute. I don't know where you got the idea that I tried to commit suicide, but you're all wrong. So if it's all the same to you, I'd like to get my things so that I can get out of here. Everybody in this place must be outpatients from the local insane asylum, including you."

I was on the verge of screaming and had a very difficult time controlling myself.

He threw his hands up in the air. I thought he was going to hit me.

Instead, he said, "You know young lady, you're right. I am crazy for not having you put in jail when they first told me about all the trouble you caused. But, no, like a fool, I let Marie talk me into giving you a break. She's the one who convinced everyone that you weren't on drugs. She even had me believing that you were some poor little victim who tried to end it all because things were tough. Look honey, the hamburger's on me. Just get your things and get your little tail out of here."

There was a long and very uncomfortable silence. I heard myself speaking. I sounded surprisingly calm.

"Is Marie the waitress who waited on me this afternoon?"

My voice was almost a whisper. I felt weak. Not sick like before, but weak. So much had happened and I wasn't able to think straight. Although, I was very grateful to Marie for sparing me the embarrassment of going to jail. I repeated my question.

"Is Marie the waitress who waited on me this afternoon?"

There was a slight pause. When he answered, his voice came out gruff. The way it was earlier.

"Yeah, she's the waitress."

"Well, I'd like to see her before I go. I'd like to thank her for sticking up for me without even knowing who I am."

I was shaking, but my voice did not betray me.

When he replied, some of the gruffness had disappeared.

"I'm afraid that won't be possible. Marie goes off duty at seven o'clock."

Seven o'clock. I had no idea that it was so late. I must have been in here for the whole day. I reached for my bags. When I found my wallet, I pulled out five dollars.

"I hope this will be enough to pay for the hamburger and soda that I ordered."

For the first time, he seemed relaxed. He shook his head in disbelief and said, "I'll tell you what. Why don't you put your money away and let me treat you to a real dinner ... on the house?"

I started to refuse his offer. Then I remembered that I really hadn't eaten anything all day. I was hungry enough to eat two meals. So, I agreed.

"I can't call you Young Lady forever, now can I? I'm Steven Gerrard, but you can call me Steve."

He was smiling now. He certainly did change his tune quickly enough.

"My name is Irene Sommers, but you can call me Miss Sommers." I said lightly.

He chuckled a little, then made an exaggerated bow and said, "All right Miss Sommers, lets go. Would you like to drop your things off at your hotel first?"

"Yes, as a matter of fact I would." I answered.

I may as well kill two birds with one stone I thought to myself. Since I had no choice in the matter now anyway. I had to take Sam's advice and stay at a hotel until I could find an apartment. So, I admitted to Steve that I had to find a hotel first, preferably one that wasn't too expensive. I was relieved when he told me that he knew just the place.

As we walked to his car, I got a good look at him. He really wasn't half bad. Not that he was handsome or anything, but he wasn't the pits either. Things were beginning to look up.

The hotel was quite a distance from the diner, and I felt a little guilty for making Steve go through the trouble. Especially after the afternoon that had just passed. Since it was so late, I decided to freshen up a little. I put on a dress and fixed my hair. By this time it had dried. I was glad that I had naturally curly hair, because with the new casual look of today, I managed to get myself together in less than my usual hour and a half.

When I entered the lobby where Steve was waiting for me, I felt like my old self again. I must have looked pretty good too, because when he saw me, he gave me a complementary wolf whistle. He stood up grinning, "I almost didn't recognize you. You're a knock-out, you know that?"

"Why thank you kindly." I said in my flirty voice.

We walked out smiling at each other. A typical couple on a date. If only people knew the real story. It was as if we shared a very funny secret. The thought of this made me laugh to myself. Steve looked at me and said, "What are you thinking about?"

When I told him what was on my mind, we both laughed. He had a good sense of humor. I might have a nice time after all.

We did have a nice time. In fact we had a wonderful time. Steve turned out to be the perfect date. He was full of surprises too. First of all, I had expected to return to the diner for dinner, but I noticed that we headed in another direction outside the city. When I asked Steve where we were going, he cocked his eyebrow and said, "I invited you to dinner and that's where I'm taking you, Miss Sommers."

"If I recall correctly, you invited me to dinner on the house. So, naturally I assumed that you meant we were dining at your restaurant."

"We are dear lady, we are."

I turned to look at him then. "Are you having another one of your seizures again? Because if you are, count me out of this one, O.K.?"

"I guess you don't like surprises, so I had better explain." He was still smiling.

His explanation was simple enough. Steve did own the diner that I was in earlier, but he also owned another establishment outside of the city. He was in partnership with his two brothers. They owned the diner in the city, the place that we were going to now, and a hamburger hut in North Jersey. I was impressed, but I tried not to show it.

Soon, we entered the parking lot of the Exquisite Delight Restaurant. I was flabbergasted. It was nice, very nice indeed. I was glad that I had changed my clothes.

Dinner was great, with cocktails and all. The whole works. I was treated like a queen. I met Steve's older brother, Ron. He was a little taller and heavier than Steve, but the strong family resemblance was unmistakable. What really topped the evening off was the way that Steve made me feel. He acted like he really thought I was something special. Like when he asked Ron, "Can I pick 'em or can I pick 'em?" Then he glanced at me and winked. I glowed. I wondered if later, he would tell Ron how we really became dinner partners.

We left the restaurant a little after eleven. I didn't realize how tired I was until we were in the car on the way to my hotel. I couldn't keep my eyes open. We were riding along, and the next thing I knew, we were parked in the lot of my hotel, and the motor of the car was turned off. I had fallen asleep. I opened my eyes, and looked up to see Steve staring at me intently. I was embarrassed that I had fallen asleep.

"I'm sorry I fell asleep on you like this, I must have been more tired than I thought, with my trip this morning and my busy afternoon. Those drinks at dinner didn't help matters any either." I rambled on and on. As I talked, I wondered just how long we had been parked here, and how long he had been looking at me sleeping.

I gave a nervous laugh and said, "You know I don't usually fall asleep on people like this. Maybe I'd better go inside, because I'm very tired."

Steve seemed amused by my embarrassment. A smile creased his face. "Don't apologize, he said, I enjoyed every minute of it. His smile broadened. "Do you know that you make little humming noises while you're sleeping?"

Now he was making fun of me, I thought. Whatever I did when I was asleep was a very personal matter. I told him that I had better call it a night, and thanked him again for such a nice evening. I had my hand on the door handle, ready to open it when he reached over my lap and took my hand in his and just held it for a few seconds. Oh brother, I thought, now for the big payoff. I should have known that he was going to want some kind of payment for all the trouble he went through for me tonight. The women he knew probably fell on their faces for him anyway. After all he wasn't too bad looking and was pretty well off to boot. I became angry. If he thought I could be bought with a dinner, he had another think coming. I yanked my hand out of his and said, "Good-night, Mr. Gerrard."

He looked a little hurt, but made no attempt to touch me again.

"Wait a minute before you go inside, he said, When am I going to see you again? Are you going to be busy tomorrow?"

I thought for a moment. The way I felt, I could sleep all day tomorrow. However, I also knew that I was going to have to get busy with finding myself a job and a place to stay. I couldn't afford this hotel room for long.

"I'll be very busy tomorrow with getting myself settled here. I have to find a job, and I'm still in the market for an apartment. So I should have my hands pretty full for a while. But, I want to thank you again for a lovely evening and all your help. You were a life saver."

Steve waved his hand dismissing my last statement. "Listen, you're going to have to stop for a break sometime, so, I'll give you a call tomorrow night around seven. We'll work things out from there, O.K.?"

I was flattered, but at the same time I felt a twinge of apprehension because I found myself attracted to him and I liked the attention he gave me. I didn't want him to think that I was just another easy mark. If we had met under different circumstances, things would have been less complicated.

Since he's the one who suggested we see each other again, I reasoned, and since I really wanted to see him again, I told him that I would be delighted if he called me tomorrow at seven. I talked myself into it.

He said, "Good, that's settled."

Then he turned, opened the door on his side of the car, and got out. I was surprised when the passenger door opened. He held it open for me to get out. He really knew how to treat a person. I can honestly say that I enjoyed all the attention he gave me.

Steve walked with me through the lobby to the elevator. My room was on the fifth floor. When the elevator door opened, he touched my cheek with his fingers and said, "Until seven, Miss Sommers." I got on the elevator, and as I rode up to my floor, I thought of the way his voice sounded when he said, "Until seven ..."

I had no trouble falling to sleep that night. When I awoke in the morning, I felt as if I could conquer the world. My thoughts were filled with Steve. I wasn't even nervous when I went on my first job interview. I had ordered the local newspaper from the desk clerk at the hotel. While I had my breakfast, I circled every job that looked promising.

I made three calls from the hotel to set up job interviews for myself. All of the locations were in the downtown area. That was good, because although I didn't know how to travel that well, I did get a chance to see a little of the downtown area yesterday. I felt confident. I guess my positive attitude paid off because the second interview ended with my landing the job. It was for a shipping firm that handled office supplies. My duties would consist of general office work. Filing, light bookkeeping and very little typing. I shared the office with two other women. Mrs. Gaynor, who insisted I call her Ruth, explained that they were like a family there because the firm was small. Everyone knew each other and got together twice a year with their families. That sounded nice to me since my family was all the way in South Jersey. Connie, the other girl was a little older than myself, about twenty six. She had been working there for six years, and from her conversation, I gathered that she enjoyed her job very much. Everything was working out perfectly. Now all I needed was an apartment. I mentioned this to Ruth and Connie. They told me that Mr. Robert Graham, our boss, had a brother in real estate. When he brought the usual papers for me to fill out, I mentioned that I needed help in finding an apartment. He set up an appointment for the next day for me to meet with his brother. I could hardly believe that things were going along so smoothly, especially after the events of yesterday. I didn't want to think about yesterday. I wanted to think about last night and Steve. I was excited about telling him how good my day went. I wanted to rush to seven o'clock.

I felt so good about seeing Steve, that I decided to splurge and buy myself a new outfit to wear. I stopped off at one of the downtown stores and bought a powder blue dress and navy blue shoes and purse. To accent the dress, I picked out a multicolored scarf. I got home in just enough time to get myself ready before seven. When the telephone rang at about six-fifty, my heart jumped. It was Steve. He asked if I would be able to go out with him. That maybe we could have dinner or something. I told him yes, and that I had a surprise for him. Two minutes after I had spoken with him on the telephone, there was a knock on my door. That couldn't possibly be him already. I asked, "Who is it?" When I heard his voice, I had to control myself from flinging the door open.

"How did you get here so fast?" I asked. He smiled sheepishly answering that he had made the call from the lobby downstairs. I was so glad to see him, but I pretended to pout and said, "I don't know if I like the idea of you being so sure of me. Suppose I had something else to do?. Suppose I had another date? You can't just take a woman for granted, you know."

He put his face very close to mine. I could feel his breath on my cheek. Then he said, "If she's my woman, I can. And you Miss Sommers, had better get used to me being around."

His words made me tingle. His breath. His body so close to mine. I was hooked. There was no way that I could act coy or indifferent now. I know it's crazy, but I was falling in love with a man that I had met only yesterday. But, that's the way it should be, isn't it? Fireworks, trumpets, drum rolls all wrapped up in one beautiful package.

I turned slowly, brushing my face against his mouth. We were facing each other. Our lips touching lightly. I closed my eyes for the expectant kiss, but I felt him move slightly. I opened my eyes. Steve was looking at me smiling. I blinked, partially from embarrassment. I tried to turn away from his steady gaze, but he cupped my chin in his hands and whispered, "Later, my love, later." Then almost as if we'd never shared that moment, he said in his usual teasing voice, "Well, what's all this about a surprise you have for me?"

I had to think for a minute, back on the days events to understand what he was talking about. Then it all came back to me. I became excited again. When I told Steve about my new job and my appointment with Mr. Grahams brother for an apartment, he acted really surprised and happy. According to him, I had accomplished a great feat. All night long I was his, "Spunky Babe", or his "Little Lady". I was in paradise. I was Steve's woman, and everything was perfect. My thoughts echoed his words, "Later my love, later."

We didn't dine at the Exquisite Delight Restaurant. Steve took me to a smaller more secluded restaurant in the city. I asked him why we didn't have dinner in one of his restaurants. His reply was simply that he wanted to have me all to himself tonight, without any interference.

The intimacy of the little place took on a very special meaning to me. This was "our place", Steve's and mine.

"... Later my love, later ..."

During dinner we got to know each other. I told him about Tina, Sam and the kids, and how my life had been up to this point. That didn't take very long. Until then, I didn't realize just how dull and uneventful my life had been. Now I understood my restlessness of the past few months.

Steve told me about his family. How he and his brothers got involved in the restaurant business. His family was large, and very close-knit. There were five brothers and two sisters. Steve was somewhere in the middle. Two of his brothers and a sister lived on the west coast. The other sister lived in Chicago with her family. I felt as if I'd know him all my life.

Finally, we were on our way back to my hotel room. I walked from the car, through the lobby and into the elevator on a cloud. We reached the fifth floor. I handed Steve the key to my room I didn't trust my shaking hands. Anticipation of what was to come made me nervous. This was a good nervousness.

Steve and I entered the dark room We closed the door behind us. We didn't need the light to see. We didn't need anything except each other. I felt Steve's body grow tense as his arms encircled me. He bent down and kissed my neck, tiny little kisses trailing from my ear to the space between my neck and shoulder. His breath was hot and urgent. Between each kiss he murmured, "Baby, You're my woman, you're really my woman now." My heart soared. My body rejoiced as Steve's touch awakened all my senses. He seemed familiar with every part of me.

Steve carried me effortlessly to the waiting bed. He undressed me with expert skill. His fingers caressed the inside of my trembling thighs, starting from my knees, making tiny circles moving upward to the designated mark. By this time my blood was coursing wildly through my veins. His fingers approaching closer and closer, making it impossible for me to keep still. I began to moan, urging him onward. He placed his body above mine. His magic fingers found the moist groove between my legs. Then he lowered his body and I felt the hardness of him just before he entered me. My breath stopped. Everything stopped except the sensation that I was feeling. We were both moaning now, caught up in a passionate whirl-wind, where reality becomes only sharing, sighing teasing, touching ... it was wonderful.

I couldn't believe my life had taken such a turn for the better. I had my new life, my job and my man. Mr. Right. All within one week. I was happy.

I was at my desk sorting the mail, when Mr. Graham approached me with a cheery, "Good-Morning." He told me that his brother was stopping by in a few minutes on a personal matter, and that after they were finished, perhaps I could take the rest of the morning off to check on the apartments that he had found for me. Mr. Graham seemed very concerned. I liked his sincere manner.

Carl Graham was much younger that I'd expected. In fact if I didn't know better, I would have taken him for his older brother's son. He had a very friendly way about himself. You know, the kind of person who doesn't meet a stranger. He was very good at his business too. I only looked at one apartment, and fell in love with it immediately. It was within my price range, not too far from the subway and just right for me. Although it was on the third floor, I had my own entrance, and a balcony from my living room window. I made arrangements to move that week.

The rest of the day was a breeze. I whizzed through my clerical chores and enjoyed the conversation and the office antics. Ruth and Connie were a lot of fun to work with.

At four-thirty on the dot, Steve appeared in the doorway of my office. I had just tidied-up and was ready to leave. I introduced him to everyone and we left. He took me straight to my hotel room, explaining that he had to take a trip to New Jersey on business. I was glad that he hadn't planned anything, because I wanted to give Tina and Sam a call to tell them my good news. Steve gave me a quick kiss at the elevator and said that he'd make it up to me tomorrow. I watched him as he walked through the lobby. "My Guy!" The thought made me tingle.

Sam and Tina were happy to hear of my success in finding a job and an apartment so soon. Mike, Richie and Linda kept interrupting to talk to me. It was good to hear their voices.

Finally Tina and I had a few moments alone. So, I told her about Steve. She seemed a little hesitant, and reserved, so I didn't pursue that line of conversation any further. Besides, once she and Sam met Steve, they would see that they had nothing at all to worry about. We talked for a few minutes longer, and Tina made me promise to call them as soon as I got settled in my apartment. She was smart enough not to offer to help me with anything. I knew how hard that must have been for her.

Things went along well for the next few weeks. I moved into my apartment. My job flourished and Steve was very attentive. I had everything.

After I had been living away from home for about two months, I decided to pay my family a visit. I was beginning to miss them. Also, I figured that this would be a good time for Tina and Sam to meet Steve. Our relationship wasn't moving along quite fast enough to suit me. I thought that by this time, we would have at least gotten to the "talking about the future" stage. I was beginning to change my views on marriage. With Steve as a husband, marriage seemed like the most sensible thing to do. Only, as I said before, our relationship was at a standstill. Maybe, if he saw how happy Tina and Sam were, he'd be prompted to pop the question.

My new life kept me pretty busy. The only thing that bothered me was that Steve didn't seem to want to be a part of this side of my life. When we were together, we either dined at the Exquisite Delight, or at some little dinner like the one he took me to on our second date. I'd asked him repeatedly to take me to the place he owned in New Jersey, but he always had some kind of excuse. I never did get to go there. So, you can understand my excitement at the idea of us visiting Tina and Sam. I made all sorts of plans. I picked out just the right outfit to wear. I knew that I looked my best in blue.

Steve wasn't too cooperative. It was only after several requests that he agreed to go. We were to leave at nine o'clock Saturday morning.

I was all dressed and ready to go at eight-thirty. I waited. Nine o'clock came and went. By ten-thirty, I was frantic.

What if he's had an accident? What if he's somewhere trying to reach me and can't? The ringing of the telephone broke into my thoughts. It was Steve. Thank heavens, he was all right.

His voice sounded a little strange. His words were strained. He told me that something very important had come up and that I should go to my sisters as planned. He was to call me at my apartment at eleven o'clock this evening. Before I had a chance to answer, I heard the telephone click in my ear.

I went to Tina's alone. They didn't even ask about Steve, or why he didn't come with me. I was so worried about Steve and what he had to tell me at eleven o'clock, that I wasn't very good company. I think Tina and Sam understood. When I said that I had to leave early, they didn't question me. Before I left, Tina looked at me for a moment and said, "Call me when you get home, and take care of yourself." She was going to say something else, but the kids interrupted to get their good-bye kisses.

Back home, I was alone with my thoughts. Eleven o'clock seemed like years away instead of just two hours. I didn't know what to do with myself. I turned on the radio and tried to relax. I dozed off to the sound of "Marvin Gaye" belting out a song. The next thing I knew, sunlight was streaming through the slits in my venetian blinds. The announcer on the radio was saying something about, "Finding greater peace with Jesus".

Sunday morning? Had I slept through my eleven o'clock call? Of course not. I would have heard the telephone ring. Steve didn't call at all. I'd slept the night through. What was I going to do? It dawned on me that I didn't know how to get in touch with Steve other than the restaurant. He'd never given me his address or his home phone number. Then I thought of his brother Ron, at the Exquisite Delight Restaurant. I looked at the clock. Seven-forty-five am. It was too early to call, so I decided to take a shower and get dressed, just in case Steve surprised me by coming to my apartment with an explanation. I had my doubts about that. Something was radically wrong. I could sense it.

After I dressed, I fixed myself breakfast and settled down with the Sunday newspaper.

I waited until about two o'clock in the afternoon before I called Ron. Deep down I was hoping that Steve would show up.

I could tell by the sounds of the restaurant, that it was very busy. When Ron finally did pick up the receiver, I got the impression that my call was slightly annoying. He just said that he'd give Steve the message that I had called. Right before I hung up the receiver, I thought I heard Steve's voice in the background laughing. Now, I was becoming paranoid. I had to think. To clear my head. This waiting for something to happen, yet not knowing what that something is, was driving me crazy.

I decided to go to the movies. I checked the listings to see what was playing. I was all set and ready to go when I changed my mind. what if Steve called while I was away. He had never stood me up like this before. Whatever the problem was, it had to be very urgent for him not to at least contact me. I waited.

Sunday turned to Monday. I went to work as usual. For a short while I was able to think about something else besides my problems. I was glad that I had gotten to know Ruth and Connie so well.

I went straight home after work, hoping that Steve would be there when I arrived. He wasn't. By this time, my concern was rapidly changing to anger.

Monday night was a little easier to handle. I even found myself getting interested in a television program. I was still on pins and needles, but I guess I just got used to the feeling.

When I didn't hear from Steve by Tuesday, I thought about calling the restaurant again, but after my last call, I gave up on that idea. It probably wouldn't have done much good anyway.

I had just turned the key in the lock Wednesday evening after a fairly easy day on the job, when I heard my telephone ringing. It was Steve. The sound of his voice almost made me forget my anger. I was a little surprised at how calm he sounded. He apologized for the last four days, saying that his business took an unexpected turn, and that he had to go out of town to take care of it. He said that he had just gotten back and was calling from a phone booth at Grand Central Station. With the little pride that I had left, I was going to tell him that I had plans for the evening, and that I couldn't possibly see him tonight. Before I could get a word out, I heard him say, "Sorry, I can't see you tonight, Babe, but I'm a little tired from the trip. So, I'll get some rest, and be at my top form for you tomorrow night. He ended with, "I've really missed being with you, Babe, see you tomorrow night, O.K.?"

I didn't know whether to laugh or cry. I just said, "O.K. Steve", and hung up. There went my last ounce of self respect. I could have curled up and died.

All day Thursday I kept thinking about my conversation with Steve. His attitude annoyed me. I just didn't understand how he could have changed so much. Or, had he really changed at all? Was I just blinded by my own desires? Was I the kind of person who saw only what I wanted to see?

Steve was waiting for me when I got home. He acted as if nothing had changed. He was his familiar charming self, making plans for the evening. He even had the nerve to suggest that we make it an early night, because he wanted to be alone with me to make up for the past few days.

We went to "Our place", but it wasn't the same. Nothing was the same, not even Steve. His suggestive remarks and possessive attitude didn't have the same meaning as before. Somehow I didn't feel like "His Woman" any more. I didn't feel protected. I didn't feel loved. I didn't feel anything except shame. Did everybody know all along, what I just realized this evening? Was everybody laughing at me through their politeness? Was Steve laughing at me when I agreed so quickly to go out with him? Was he laughing at me when I accepted what I thought was kindness on his part? Was he laughing at me when I said I loved him? Was he laughing at me when I allowed him to make love to me? All these thoughts were going through my head. I wasn't hungry anymore. I just wanted to go home.

When I looked at him to tell him that I wanted to leave, suddenly, Steve wasn't Steve. Not the Steve that I was in love with. Not the Steve of my imagination. He seemed much older. I realized that I had never even asked his age. In fact there were a lot of things that I didn't know about him. For instance, where he lived, or with whom. Why was I never introduced to any of his family except Ron? What was the big secret concerning his place in New Jersey? Why didn't we have any mutual friends.

Steve saw me looking at him. I must have been staring because he gave a nervous laugh, and said, "A penny for your thoughts, Baby Cakes."

"Do you really want to know my thoughts, Steve? Do you really want to know?"

I think I knew the answer to my next question before I even asked it. But, I had to hear the answer from him.

"Are you married Steve? Is that why you have so many secrets from me?" I watched him closely.

The muscle in his jaw jumped. His eyes moved from side to side, as if his mind were searching for an answer.

He answered me without uttering a word. I couldn't stand being there with him any longer. This *Old man*. How could I have been so gullible. So stupid.

I stood up and said as calmly as I could, "Good-bye Steve." I turned and walked out of the restaurant.

I don't even know how I got home. I was in a daze. After I changed into my nightgown, I telephoned Tina. I needed to talk to someone. We talked for nearly two hours. Tina didn't ask what the problem was. My sister is a very wise woman. We talked about everything, even things that happened when we were children.

I invited her, Sam and the kids to my house for Sunday dinner. She made a joke about not having to cook for a change, and said, "See you Sunday, Sissy." She hadn't called me Sissy in years. Not since I made a big project about being a grown woman on my eighteenth birthday.

"Bye, Tina, kiss Sam and the kids for me." I ended the conversation feeling sad, but a little less alone. I turned on the radio and tried to relax.

The telephone rang about two-thirty in the morning and then again about three-fifteen. I knew that it was Steve, so I just let it ring. We had nothing else to discuss.

Steve never tried to get in touch with me again. I guess I wasn't important enough to him.

This all happened six months ago. I'm still a little bitter about being made a fool of, but I guess that's all part of growing up. I realize now that at twenty-one, I still have a long way to go.

I don't have a steady male friend, but I do date occasionally. I've found out that Connie and I have a lot in common. She's introduced me to a lot of the attractions of the city that I didn't know before. I spend at least one week-end a month with my family in South Jersey. I don't feel threatened anymore by Tina's apron strings. In fact, I'm happy for them.

Yesterday, I thought I saw a familiar face in the crowd while walking to the store. I felt a sudden ache in my chest, but when I turned, I saw no one that I knew. Only strangers. I composed myself and went on my merry way

I'm not completely over my bad experience, but I'm taking each day, one day at a time. After all, I'm young, I'm pretty and I have my whole life ahead of me.

The End

8

And Out of My Past

We left our favorite night club a little after one in the morning. Rita, Lisa and I were all getting tired of the singles scene. But, here we were, like clockwork, every Saturday night, doing our own thing , along with millions of other young people. All of us searching for something. Something that always seems to be just beyond our reach.

The three of us were friends in high school. And now six years after graduation, we are still friends. Rita and I have office jobs and Lisa is a beautician. I guess we are happy with our career choices, but then again we know that there is something missing. Romance, love and marriage. Of course, we have our share of dates and men but nothing lasting, nothing permanent.

"Hey Pam!" Rita called out to me. Where's our friend? He's not in his regular spot."

My eyes were drawn to the familiar spot in the alleyway. I knew she was talking about the drunkard who for the past four months was either slouching or lying in one of the store fronts as we passed each Saturday night on our way to where we'd parked our car. We'd gotten so used to seeing that pitiful man in the doorway. We even made harmless jokes about him. That's how we began calling him our friend.

It was strange not seeing him this night and I was just about to speak on that fact when we heard it. At first it was a low moaning sound that came from the darkness behind the corner building. Then the sound grew louder and louder until we could make out the meaning of it's words.

"Help me! Dear Lord ... Help me."

Lisa, Rita and I stared at one another not knowing what to do. Something moved from the darkness into the light, stumbled and fell almost in front of our feet. It was the drunkard ... *Our Friend*. Only now he seemed to be more in pain than drunk.

Suddenly, Lisa screamed, "Look at his leg!".

We looked. There was blood on his soiled trousers. So much of it that you couldn't tell where the actual wound was. And from the position of his foot, it was obvious that his leg was broken because it was terribly twisted. We had to get help. Luckily, there was a telephone booth on the corner. Rita called the police emergency.

Within minutes a police car arrived followed by a hospital ambulance. I saw the attendants lift *our friend* onto the stretcher and carry him to the ambulance. As they passed by, the man touched my arm and said, "Thank you."

It wasn't what he said, but the sound of his voice that made me look at him. His face, his eyes. I kept looking at him. I couldn't seem to stop myself. What was it, I questioned myself. Why was I so drawn to this poor man? My mind was racing and I didn't even know why. All I could concentrate on was his face, his eyes, his voice. Especially his voice.

It's a good thing that Lisa was driving her car that night instead of me because I couldn't get my thoughts to connect with anything other than that poor man. I was terribly disturbed by him. Even more so, I was baffled as to why I was so disturbed by him.

It was about 2:30 in the morning when I finally got home. For the first time since I'd moved out of my mothers house three years ago, I wished that she was sitting up waiting for me the way she always did when I lived at home. Instead, I walked up the three flights and entered my empty apartment.

I showered and dressed for bed, all the while thinking. My thoughts were jumbled, mixed up. Today, tonight, yesterday and things in the past were all muddled, rattling around chaotically in my head.

I fell into a fitful sleep.

I awoke with a start. Suddenly, everything was crystal clear. I knew what it was that was puzzling me. All the pieces fit. That face. Those eyes. That voice. Yesterday, today ... everything!

I knew exactly what I had to do.

The Beth-Israel Medical Center was located on the other side of town from where I lived. I was surprised that it only took me twenty minutes to get there.

I recognized him as soon as I entered the pristine hospital room. My heart jumped. He was all cleaned up. His hair was brushed and except for the stubble, his unshaved face looked the same as I remembered. I felt, as I neared his bed, that I was walking into my past.

"Mr. Chadson?"

I said his name for the first time in many years. He turned abruptly, but didn't say anything. He just stared. He was still quite handsome. I began to get nervous. Maybe this wasn't such a hot idea after all. But I couldn't turn back now.

"You *are* Mr. Chadson, Mr. Brian Chadson, aren't you?" My voice cracked.

After what seemed like an eternity, he said, "Yes, I am." The words came out quietly, barely above a whisper. He continued to look at me. His expression was one gigantic question mark.

I felt as if I were back in high school, giddy and up-tight. Everything came to me in a rush. My emotions were ignited by my memories. This was Mr. Chadson, my favorite high school teacher.

His probing stare prompted me to answer.

"Mr. Chadson, I know you probably don't remember me." My words tumbled out.

"But, I was in your English class my Junior year in high school." I continued, barely taking a breath. "When my friends and I saw you last night ..."

He turned away at that statement, but I couldn't stop talking.

"...When I saw you last night, I felt there was something familiar in your voice, your eyes or something. I don't know, but this morning, when I woke up, it dawned on me just who you were and I decided that I would come to see how you made out and ... well, how's your leg? Are you all right? ... You look just fine, all cleaned up and everything ..." My voice trailed off.

He turned to face me again. I'd finally run out of things to say. I felt stupid, and wished I'd stopped talking before I'd embarrassed myself. Only now, I just stood there with a lump in my throat and my foot in my mouth, waiting for him to punch me in the nose or something.

I was relieved when he smiled and said, "I *feel* better too. And, yes, my leg is all right. They patched it up pretty good for me."

He threw the cover back. His leg was bandaged from hip to ankle. I wondered what could have happened to have caused this much damage. I was curious but afraid to ask. There was silence again. He was obviously uncomfortable and I just didn't know what to do next.

Finally, he gave a little sigh and started talking. He told me that he'd climbed on top of the boxes in the alley to test the window of the building. Not to steal anything but for shelter. He just wanted to sleep inside the building. He stumbled and fell, breaking his leg on the way down. There was broken glass where he'd landed. That's why there was so much blood. His words were strained. I could tell he was embarrassed.

Thank goodness the nurse interrupted our discomfort. She informed Mr. Chadson that he'd be able to leave the hospital at any time. Again, uncomfortable silence permeated the room. The nurse unaware that there was anything wrong turned and left.

I don't know what came over me, but all of a sudden I found myself taking charge. The next thing I knew, Mr. Chadson was dressed in the dirty rags he'd worn the night before and we were sitting in my car.

Now what? He had no place to go ... so, I took him home with me. I was surprised that he'd come along so willingly. Then again, there was nothing much he could do with his broken leg. He could hardly get around, even with my helping him.

After we struggled the three agonizing flights to my apartment, I began to get a little nervous about what I'd gotten myself into. Then I remembered that this was Mr. Chadson. He couldn't be that much different from the way he was when he was teaching school. All the kids liked him. He always had something encouraging to say and he was a very good teacher too. I convinced myself that I had made the right decision. I was merely helping Mr. Chadson, and what could possibly be wrong with that?

Only one thing still disturbed me. I was puzzled. What could have happened in his life to make him give up on everything? What could have happened in his life to make him become a *bum?*

His words broke into my thoughts as if he were able to read my mind.

"I gave up teaching." He volunteered. "Two years ago. Something happened. I couldn't teach anymore. I couldn't do anything anymore."

That was all he said. Only the far away look on his face told me that whatever happened two years ago must have been very horrible to do this to him. My God, he'd sunk about as low as a person could go.

He became very quiet. He seemed tired and in need of rest. I knew the first thing I had to do was to get rid of those dirty, torn clothes he was wearing. The only things I had that could fit him were my old jogging suits, sweat shirts and pants. I took his tattered clothing and with his permission, I threw them into the garbage. We'd just have to figure out a way to get him something more suitable to wear later. For now, at least, he had a clean change of clothes.

Brian, as he insisted I call him, slept through the afternoon. My living room couch converted into a bed which helped my new situation considerably.

When Brian awoke, we had dinner. It was then that I found out what had happened to him. Two years ago, Brian's entire family, his father, mother and younger sister died in a car accident. Brian escaped with barely a scratch. He was driving the car. Poor Brian.

For two years he carried the guilt of that fatal night. In his mind, he had murdered his family, the people who meant the most to him in the world. I know it sounds strange, but after Brian told me the story of what happened to him, we seemed to share a closeness. A bond that was stronger than anything I'd ever felt before with anyone.

The next three months were like something out of a dream. At first when everyone found out about Brian living in my apartment, I got a lot of opposition. Especially from my mother. But, when they found out how determined I was to help him, they accepted the idea. Or at least they didn't continue to badger me about it.

Rita and Lisa were upset because with Brian in my life, our Saturday night dates were out of the question. I didn't care. Now I had plenty to do to keep myself occupied. Besides, for the first few weeks Brian was awfully sick. I didn't know it then, but I found out later that his sickness was caused by his body's withdrawal from all the alcohol he'd consumed.

One day I came home from work expecting to find him in his usual spot, either sitting or lying on the couch. I was surprised to find the couch empty and the living room was spotless. In fact, my entire apartment was spotless. I finally found Brian in the kitchen limping around adding the final touches to a spaghetti dinner that he'd spent the whole afternoon preparing. He looked better than I'd seen him looking in a long time, rested and clean shaven. He even had a little color to his complexion. He admitted to waking up this morning feeling, as he put it, *"great"*. So, he went on to explain that he ordered some very much needed groceries and prepared dinner as a surprise for me. I wondered where he'd gotten the money for the groceries, but I was so overwhelmed and delighted by everything else that I didn't say anything. I just enjoyed the moment.

Brian was so funny trying to be gallant while hobbling around on his broken leg. He couldn't even stand up straight, much less bow and help me to my seat. However, he made a sincere effort to do so, almost spilling our dinner in the process.

We did the dishes together. It took twice as long with Brian helping, but it was fun.

Later, we settled down in front of the television set. Neither one of us paid much attention to what was on the screen. We laughed and talked about everything and reminisced about the good old days. It was hard to believe that just a few short weeks ago this clean shaven, witty man with his boyish grin was a bum in the streets.

All of a sudden, Brian became quiet and serious. He looked at me with piercing eyes that I could not look away from. I was drinking soda. He reached down and took the glass from my trembling hand and placed it on the coffee table in front of us. I knew he was going to kiss me and I did nothing to stop him. I didn't want to stop him. I wanted him to kiss me and when he did, it was sweet and long, growing in intensity. When he pulled away, his body was tense. I could tell he was fighting with himself for control. He began to speak. his words were deliberately slow as if making sure I understood their meaning fully. My head was spinning.

"Pam", he said, "aren't you in the least bit curious as to where I got the money to buy groceries and our spaghetti dinner?"

Of course I was curious, but right now, that wasn't my main concern. I simply said, "Yes Brian, I'm curious."

"These last few weeks"' he said, "have given me a different outlook. You believed in me, Pam, when I didn't believe in myself."

At this point, he took a deep breath, then continued. "I'm a fairly wealthy man. I have money that's done nothing but gain interest for the past two years. When I acquired this money, Pam, I vowed that I would never spend one red cent of it. I couldn't stand the way it came to me. I didn't want it. I didn't deserve it ..."

I looked at him then and saw such deep hurt that I put my fingers to his lips. He didn't have to explain any further. I understood how he felt about the insurance money from the death of his family.

Brian pressed my fingers closer to his lips, kissed each of them, then pulled my hand away and covered it with both of his.

"It's all right now. I want to live again. I want to do something for someone, for *you*, Pam. I want ..." He seemed to run out of words as he pulled me towards him and kissed me again. This time letting go completely. His passion mounting, his ardor engulfing me, sending tiny explosions that surged throughout my inflamed body. I surrendered joyously and completely.

From that time on, life for me was wonderful. I went to work each day on a cloud, knowing that I would be returning home to Brian. Home was a happy place for me. I was not alone.

Each day I could see improvement in Brian's recovery. His stumble became a limp and he didn't grimace as much from pain as he did in the beginning.

My days were filled with thoughts of Brian and my nights were even better because Brian was there. I was happy. I knew Brian loved me as much as I loved him. Sometimes I'd catch him staring at me and I was sure that he was thinking of a way to ask me to marry him. When he didn't, I was disappointed. I just waited for the time that he would propose. I was certain it would happen sooner or later.

We talked a lot and laughed a lot and we loved a lot. I remember once, we even cried together. It was the day that we found out that Brian would always have occasional pain in his leg and walk with a limp. He used a cane sometimes to help him walk around, but most of the time he didn't need it.

Rita and Lisa visited us on Sundays. If they ever suspected that Brian and I were more than just friends, they never said anything.

Since Brian insisted on *taking over*, I was able to save most of my paycheck each week. With my extra money, I planned a big surprise for Brian. A week-end trip to our local resort area was just the thing. I knew he was getting pretty tired of being stuck in the apartment most of the time. I arranged for the trip, and decided to tell Brian about it a week in advance so he could prepare for it. I was keyed up and excited at the idea of my surprise and how Brian was going to react to it. I couldn't wait to get home to tell him about it. Five o'clock finally arrived and I was the first one out of the door. I nearly flew home.

When I got home, Brian wasn't there. Oh well, I thought, my good news will have to wait until dinner time. I did wonder where he was but I wasn't alarmed because lately Brian had begun to venture out. Sometimes he'd tell me that he'd spent the whole day out doing one thing or another.

When he didn't return home by ten o'clock that evening, I was devastated. What could have happened to him? I imagined all sorts of horrible things. It didn't dawn on me that Brian wasn't coming home until the next morning after a sleepless night.

It was then that I discovered that all his belongings were gone. Brian had left me!. Dumped by a bum. I couldn't believe it. If it weren't so awful, it would have been funny. I'd never get over this humiliation. Never!

I spent the rest of the week-end in my apartment hoping that Brian would try to contact me, yet knowing in my heart that he wouldn't. He was gone and that was that. I didn't tell anyone. When Rita and Lisa came for their usual visit, I made up some excuse and got rid of them fast. I didn't feel like having company. I didn't feel like doing anything.

I went to work Monday morning. I did all the things necessary for survival. But, that was all. I was like a zombie. This went on for over a week. Stalling Rita and Lisa any longer was a lost cause. When they found out that Brian was gone and that I had wrapped myself in a cocoon of self pity, they decided that they'd have to straighten me out. Only nothing they did or suggested helped. After about three weeks of this non-existence, I let them wear down my protective wall. I agreed to go with them on Saturday night to our usual place.

So, here I was on Saturday with the whole day ahead of me before my big outing with Rita and Lisa. I decided to go shopping. It was a fairly nice day so instead of taking my car into the shopping area I took the train. That was my first mistake. The minute I sat on the seat, my mind drifted to the times when Brian and I were together and did things together. Even the small things like riding on a train was an experience. A beautiful experience. I felt a little smile lifting the corner of my mouth as I remembered the time when Brian and I, after shopping, decided to detour through the park on the way home. At the time Brian was still using crutches and was having quite a difficult time with the one package he was carrying. I was surprised when all of a sudden he placed the package on the ground and darted across the grass. I didn't know what to think until I saw him stop before a rather bedraggled old lady trying to retrieve a cart that had turned over spilling what appeared to be all of her earthly belongings onto the ground. What a sight. Brian trying to hold on to his crutch for balance, the old lady not sure what the heck he was doing, trying to protect her property from this lunatic, Brian unaware of the fact that he was scaring the little old lady with his actions. He was so engulfed with his good deed that he didn't realize the lady's dilemma until she started smacking him across the head with her canvas hand bag. By this time I was laughing so hard that they both stopped to look at me. That only made me laugh harder. When Brian realized what I was laughing at, he began to laugh. The little old lady looked from Brian to me several times before she quickly gathered her tattered belongings and practically ran away from us, glancing back now and then to make sure that Brian and I weren't following her.

"Is this the train to Rahway?"

A loud booming voice brought me back to the present. I looked up to see a very drunk disheveled man standing directly in front of me. My smile faded as I blinked to total awareness. The man repeated his inquiry for apparently I didn't respond quickly enough to suit him.

"Is this the train to Rahway?" he slurred. I answered him, confirming that yes, this was the Rahway train. I watched as he teeter tottered down the aisle.

I went out that night with the girls. Nothing had changed. I was more depressed than ever. I wanted to just curl up and die. When Lisa stopped her car in front of my apartment building, she and Rita offered to come up and keep me company for a while. They knew that I was in bad shape. I refused their offer telling them that I would be all right. Actually, the way I felt, I intended to cry myself to sleep for the rest of my life. But, I smiled and we said good-night.

I wasn't sleepy so I went into the kitchen to make myself a cup of tea. Then I decided that I really didn't want tea after all. I turned the flame off under the tea kettle and moped around the kitchen for a few moments.

I went into my bed room and turned on the light. I had to blink twice because there in the middle of my bed, fast asleep, was Brian.

"Brian!" I screeched.

He jumped and almost fell off the bed. I ran towards him then suddenly stopped. I was so happy to see him that I was about to make a fool of myself. I admit, I *did* miss him more than anything, but I had my pride too. He couldn't just come and go in my life as he pleased. I wasn't a yo-yo to be played with. I just stood there stiff and erect, glaring at him.

He smiled. I said nothing. He stood up and walked to me holding out his arms. I remained rigid.

"I guess I owe you an explanation, he said, Well, here goes. Pam, I realized that things were getting pretty serious with us a while ago but I wasn't in any position to do anything about it then because of my leg and ... you know, the other problems in my life. Now, honey, I've kind of straightened things out enough so I won't be a burden on you or any one else. I've enrolled in a program for my drinking problem." He paused, then looked directly into my eyes. "The most important part, he continued, is that I secured myself a position teaching. I'll be substituting for a while, but it looks very promising. Anyway, not that I'm practically a respectable citizen again, and can stand on my own two feet, I can do what I wanted to do before, but couldn't."

Brian was noticeably nervous. He held both my hands in his, took a deep breath and said, "Pam, I love you and I want you to be my wife. Honey, will you marry me?"

I was so hurt and angry that I saw his mouth moving but his words escaped me. All I heard was the ringing in my ears and the pounding of my own heartbeat. How dare he come back into my life after disappearing for three weeks without a word or a telephone call, and think that all would be well.

All wasn't well and I was livid. When his mouth finally stopped moving and I realized that he had paused in his speech, I exploded. I began to rant and rave, blaming him for all the injustices in the world for what he did to me and how he made me feel these past weeks.

Brian said nothing. He just kept looking at me with a silly grin on his face. I lost control. I felt like hitting him right in his smug face. As I struggled to free my hands, something clicked in my brain, similar to an after shock.

"What did you say?" I asked stupidly with my hands still in his.

His smile broadened as he raised my hands to his lips, kissing them gently. Then he placed our hands on his chest close to his heart. I felt his heart beating wildly beneath my fingers. His eyes held a steady and clear gaze.

"Will you marry me?"

I heard what he said loud and clear that time. That was all I needed. The last few weeks seemed to disappear from my memory. All I could see was a bright and beautiful future ahead of me as Brian's wife. I loved him so much at that moment, I think my heart nearly burst from happiness. I might get to treat him to that vacation after all ... for our honeymoon!

"Yes, yes!" I said as I pressed myself tightly to his body. "Yes Brian, I'll marry you."

The End

9

Today, I'm Singing the Blues

"...Yesterday at this time I sang a love song, but today, I'm singing the blues ..."

A light drizzle began to fall as tiny pellets grazed softly against the window. Inside, the bittersweet sounds emanating from the stereo filled the apartment. Amid the hue of teal and black hung a picture frame in lavish antique gold. A wedding picture. The wedding picture of Isaac and Verna Taylor.

The melody of her favorite album drifted into the bedroom. It's soulful tune penetrated the air, as the singer caressed each note with a wail, a moan, a sigh.

Verna listened. The setting was all too familiar. Her apartment was warm, cozy and plush. Just as it had been countless times in the past.

Only tonight was different. Tonight, Verna was alone. She'd come home earlier this evening to find Isaac, her husband of two years, waiting for her. His belongings were packed neatly and placed in the corner near the door.

Whatever happened to the sanctity of marriage? When did values and moral standards change so drastically?

"...Hi, Vern, ...er ... I just wanted to wait until you got home ... er ... before I leave. I ... ah ... got myself another place.

It's best this way. I ... ah ... I ... Well, anyway, I didn't want to leave without seeing you first ... "

Verna remained silent.

"I guess you'll want these." Isaac dangled the keys to the apartment in front of her.

Instinctively, Verna held out her hand, catching the keys as they fell. She didn't look at them. She saw only Isaac's face.

He gathered his things quickly, stopping to open the door. He paused for a moment.

"... Well ... Vern, Good-bye!"

Verna still looked straight ahead, frozen. She heard the door close. The lock clicked. And then nothing. Verna looked down at the keys in her hand.

"Good-bye, Isaac."

In a state of shock, Verna removed her coat. The silent, empty apartment was almost unbearable. She turned the stereo on, and walked into their bedroom. *Her* bedroom.

This all happened three hours ago. And here she still sat, on the bed, listening to the music.

Suddenly, as if for the first time, Verna heard the singer's words. The spinning record droned loudly in her ears, each note echoing her pain.

"How dare you?" she whispered.

Then she ran into the living room and stood in front of the stereo. She looked down at the spinning record.

"How dare you?" she repeated. And then louder, "How dare you invade my privacy?"

Verna felt the tears brimming in her eyes. Unable to help herself, she cried.

"How dare you sing about my private life? How dare you?"

Her voice seemed to echo as she shouted at the stereo. The record, defying her, turning, turning, while it's words continued to taunt her.

Verna stared at the record. She knew that she was being foolish. The song wasn't about her. Not really. Not personally.

Turning abruptly, she walked back into the bedroom, not even bothering to turn off the stereo.

The music could be stopped, but no one could stop the truth of it's lyrics.

The truth as it touched her. Yes, Verna was alone now, hurt and disgusted. But, others had weathered the same storm. Others had made it, had survived. In her heart, Verna knew that she would cross that bridge. Only this night, as the music played softly in the background, still holding Isaac's keys tightly in her hand ... Verna cried.

"... Yesterday at this time I sang a love song, but today, I'm singing the blues ..."

The End

About the Author

Pat Ebron (Ebony Dawn) was born in Newark, New Jersey. Her love for old films and music has helped to establish her romantic view of life. Pat has written several short stories, children's stories and plays. Now, Central New Jersey is where she calls home. Pat lives with her husband, children, grandchildren and two cats. Family has always been the main focus of Pat Ebron's life.